C

Published in the United States of America.

ISBN-13: 978-1541021327

ISBN-10: 1541021320

First paperback edition.

The characters and events portrayed in this book are fictitious.
Actual locations and brand names are used in a fictitious
context; trademarks are acknowledged, and product use or
mention in no way implies endorsement.

AnaisImprint

Miami, Florida

For my family, with love.

Fifty

Ways

to

Make

a

Family

a novel

by

k.c. wilder

Anais**Imprint**

Miami, Florida

Chapter **One**

MAY

"Ready?" Finn asked.

I shook my head.

It had taken us over an hour to hike to the ledge where we now stood, the cliff dropping off sharply at our feet, the ocean sparkling far below. I contemplated the water, wondering if it was true that, from this height, a fall into it would be like a fall onto concrete. I spotted dark shadows swimming far below. Fish? Sharks?

"Hey," Finn said, and I felt his fingertips at my chin. He tipped my face upward and leaned in. As always, I found myself reacting viscerally, drawing a deep breath that caught in my throat.

"Hey," I exhaled slowly.

The romance of the moment was broken by a jarring and clacking.

Right.

We were wearing helmets.

"You remember what we talked about, right?" he began. "I say 'go,' and you run, full steam ahead. Don't look at the cliff, just look straight ahead. Pick a spot on the horizon. I'll take care of the glider, and when we're airborne, I'll remind you to sit back and enjoy." He paused, his eyes searching mine and causing flip-flops in my belly. I never ceased to be amazed by his beauty: that chiseled jaw, those eyes—deep pools in which I could easily drown. "You're going to love this. Trust me."

I did.

I trusted him with every molecule of my being. The realization simultaneously thrilled and terrified me.

I trusted him so much, I was about to leap off a cliff with him. I was a lemming in love. This was paragliding, Finn's wild obsession, and he was about to share it with me.

He pulled back and began the countdown. My hands found the straps of my harness and traced the lines Finn had checked at least a half-dozen times. I was still stunned that all a paraglider consisted of was the wing that would rise above us and this minimal seat suspended below. It was little more than the backpacks I'd strapped onto my boys on school days past, an unsubstantial assembly of canvas and straps.

Behind us, the glider caught in the wind, rippling and pulling, jerking us forward and back before it unfurled fully. A massive sail arced high above our heads. The helmet I was wearing made it impossible to turn and take in the scene entirely. I listened to the rip of the wind in the wing, to the pounding of my heart in my chest. I was strapped into the paraglider in front of Finn, my tandem pilot.

My life was literally in his hands.

"Here we go," he said, an unmistakable edge of excitement in his voice. "Ready, Eve? Start running!"

I did as told, setting my feet in motion in the direction of the cliff. Then a strange thing happened. Something within me took over. Instinctively, I recoiled from the edge.

"Keep running, Eve," Finn cautioned, responding as my body put on the brakes.

I wanted to follow his instructions, but my feet turned to dead weight. I felt them begin to drag beneath me, the tips of my toes clinging to the cliff. I couldn't do it. I couldn't launch myself into midair from the relative safety of our perch.

I didn't have to.

Suddenly, my feet were swept out from underneath me.

"Here we go!" Finn called out, and I felt the power of his body moving behind mine, propelling us forward and over the edge.

My feet dangled in the air, my sneakers impossibly framed against the backdrop of the cascading cliffs, the rocks and sand, the sea—all of it tiny and far below. It seemed like a Photoshop job, my teal Chuck Taylors suspended in midair.

"Relax," Finn said.

I willed myself to settle into the backpack that was now my seat more than 2,000 feet above sea level. I felt Finn behind me, strapped into a backpack of his own, close enough to be comforting, though the helmets we wore made it seem we were in our own little worlds. I watched the landscape—the seascape—pass below. I tried to make sense of how surreal it looked from this height. I felt the tug of the wind at the wing above us, and I dared to look up at the canopy. The red and yellow crescent made a bold and beautiful contrast to the sky beyond. It seemed impossible that such a graceful manmade wing was the only thing keeping us from plummeting to earth.

It seemed impossible that I was here, period.

"Well? What do you think?" Finn asked.

We moved along, graceful and silent as a pair of birds, the ridge of the cliffs to our left and the deep blue of the ocean to our right. Had I ever seen such beauty? Had I ever felt more alive?

"It's breathtaking," I said truthfully. "Indescribable."

Finn leaned in close, his helmet knocking lightly against mine.

"You get it, then?" he asked. "Why I do this?"

"I get it. This is amazing."

"Look!" he said.

I followed his fingertip to the right, taking in the scene far below. A pod of dolphins leapt from the water, distant but undeniably joyous. At the risk of sounding like a total sap, a tear or two may have sprung to my eyes. I almost couldn't wrap my head around the reality of where I was and what I was doing. For so many years my life had been staid, constricting. I was a housewife, a mother, a frail bird in a gilded cage. If you'd told me a year prior that I'd find myself paragliding in South America with a gorgeous man who seemed to have eyes only for me, I'd have said you were insane.

Then again, if you'd told me any of what had happened in the past year would come to pass, I'd have said the same thing.

Insane.

Impossible.

Yet here I was.

Finn guided the wing along the coast, and we followed

the dolphins for a while. Then they switched course, heading straight out to sea, and Finn steered us back toward land. Slowly, we were descending.

"We're going to touch down over there," he said, pointing at a grassy patch at the crest of the bluff. "Same as takeoff, really. Just get your feet running, and when we make contact, keep going. Got it?"

"Yes!" I called, giving him the thumbs-up.

It sounded simple enough in theory, but much like takeoff, it didn't go as well in practice. I had one idea, my body had another. I began running while we were still airborne but closing in on the ground. Once we touched down, though, my knees buckled. Instead of running and coming gradually to a stop, I found myself in a tuck-and-roll. Finn tumbled on top of me. I felt my knees and elbows take a battering, but the damage to my ego was worse. Rough on both takeoff and landing. What the heck kind of paragliding buddy was I?

When we finally came to rest, I found Finn looking at me, a thin smile on his lips. His helmet was in his hands, his hair sweaty and askew. I bit my lip as I pulled my own helmet off, waiting for him to comment.

"So, is your nickname Grace?" he teased.

I stuck my tongue out at him.

He set our helmets down on the ground and closed his

mouth over mine. His fingertips mussed my hair. I could only imagine what I looked like at the moment, a study in helmet head and perspiration.

"It's a good thing you're cute, Eve," he whispered, his nose to mine. His eyes roamed over my face, and as always, I instinctively looked away. He brought me back with a kiss. "Ten days. We've got ten days to make a proper paragliding partner out of you."

"Will that be enough?" I laughed.

"It will have to be more than enough," he said, that sly tone I loved best creeping into his voice. "Paragliding's not the only thing I want to do with you while we're here on vacation."

I laughed and leaned into his embrace.

****

Ten days was enough.

And it wasn't.

I learned to let my body go with takeoffs, to cooperate with landings—for the most part, anyway. Before this trip, I'd had the idea that maybe I'd like to learn to paraglide solo. *Ha!* Only if I wanted to end up a stain on a beautiful landscape somewhere. Yes, I'd moved past my initial fear and learned to enjoy paragliding. I understood why Finn so loved it. But his love of paragliding was on a whole different level—and it was that love that made him so capable. While I was gazing at the landscape, in awe of the beauty of nature and our smallness within it, he was tuned in to the fine filaments of line, the wing, the wind. There was an intensity about Finn, his fixation on the mechanics of things, that I could only admire.

Finn.

I definitely admired that man, and enjoyed his boundless enthusiasm for life. When we weren't paragliding, we were snorkeling, walking the beach, swimming, kayaking, hiking.

And—*oh yes*—making love.

Sleepy and slow in the mornings, wild and playful in the afternoons, sultry and sweet late at night. Every inch of me was sore, and I loved that I couldn't tell which aching muscles or gentle bruises had come from which physical activity. Was this from yet another rough paragliding landing, or was it from an adventure in our hotel suite? The mystery thrilled me. At last I had naughty secrets concealed by my skin, this skin that had for so long seemed destined simply to age, unappreciated and practical. I wasn't sure I'd ever so fully or blissfully inhabited my body.

I tried to recall the last vacation I'd taken that didn't involve kids and beach gear and a whole lot of work on my part.

This was a brand new world. No whining, no struggle. All wild nights and lazy mornings and exploring. I had the feeling that I was learning Finn on a deeper level, he was learning me, and we both liked what we'd found.

"I love you," he said.

We were tangled together on a beach blanket in the shade of a palm.

"So you've said," I grinned, teasing.

I looked into his eyes and saw something different there. Something more solemn and still than I'd seen before.

"I love you," he said again, and I felt my breathing slow.

"I love you," I said softly.

I kissed his nose, his forehead. I paused, drawing a slow, deliberate breath. I could feel tears stinging at the corners of my eyes and I realized: *for the first time in ages, they were happy tears.* The sparkle in Finn's eyes brought a smile to my lips.

Once upon a time, not so long ago, I'd thought my world had ended.

Now, I was in love—not just in love again, but in love more deeply than I'd ever thought possible. My marriage to Skip had consumed me, obscuring my hopes and dreams. I'd since learned I was enough on my own, happy and fulfilled in my own right. But with this delightful, surprising man, I was even better.

I leaned in, pulling Finn's arms around me, pressing my body to his. I felt my toes in the sand, heard the cry of sea birds. I drew my tongue lightly across his bottom lip, tasting a mixture of salt and sunscreen. And then Finn kissed me, his hands at the small of my back, and my mind surrendered to the moment.

****

If I had any doubt that our vacation was over, the noise and bustle of the airport erased it. Finn brought coffee and pastry to me where I sat with our carry-on bags. I scrolled through the massive pileup of texts and email on my phone. I'd gladly taken Tamara's advice and left the intruding little device powered off for the entirety of the trip.

"They have a fucking phone at the resort, Eve," she'd said. "I'll call you if there's an emergency. Otherwise, forget you even have offspring. Howard and I can manage the crumb-crunching little swine."

It was advice I was glad to have taken. It may not have made me Mother of the Year, but in all honesty, after the first twenty-four hours or so, I did just about forget I even had offspring.

Now, though, the barrage of messages on my phone

brought me back to reality. There were school forms to be filled out, athletic equipment to be purchased, a vet appointment for the dog, and good news: a job interview.

"Look!" I said, smiling and holding my phone out to Finn. "The animal rescue wants me to interview with the board."

"Well, of course they do. The only reason they might possibly *not* want to hire you for shelter work is because you're already their very best volunteer coordinator."

I started to protest, but he popped a bite of pastry into my mouth, then kissed me on my sugar-coated lips.

Oh, the sweetness overload!

"I'm just going to give Tamara a quick call," I explained, tapping my phone and stepping away.

My instinctive idea had been to avoid offending those around me, but a glance back told me nearly everyone was engaged in conversation on their mobile phones. The contrast to the ten peaceful days I'd just spent unplugged was stark.

And then, there was Tam's voice.

"Well, fuck me—if it isn't the long-lost Red Fox," she teased. "Level with me: can you walk? And do you still have a pussy, or did it run away in protest after all that action?"

"Oh, Tam, you're so vulgar!" I laughed. "I've missed you! How's it going there? Have my boys been okay?"

"Well, the dog's been good as gold. Only shit on the floor once, which is far less than my own kids do. Haven't heard a damn thing from Max, so I assume all's good at Morefield. And I'm pretty sure Eli's got a girlfriend, but otherwise, nothing new."

"Wait—a girlfriend? Eli's got a girlfriend?"

My jaw hit the floor.

"Yeah, I think so. I mean, she's older, and she looks like whatsherface from *The Girl With the Dragon Tattoo*, so they're an odd fucking couple for sure, but they're awfully cozy to be 'just friends'..."

"Eli has a girlfriend...*with tattoos*?" I caught Finn looking at me from where he sat and realized I'd gotten loud, even by airport standards.

"Well, I don't think she *actually* has tattoos. She's older than Eli, but still, a little young for that," Tamara allowed. "But she has that look, you know? Moody. Goth. Bullring through the nose. Although maybe that's just a clip-on thingy."

I blinked and shook my head, as if I could somehow get the image in my mind's eye to settle in a way that made sense. Moody certainly sounded like Eli's type. But then again, was he old enough to even have a 'type?' How had I failed to realize he was at an age where a girlfriend might be a possibility?

"How did he meet her? Does she go to Pinecroft?"

"I think so. Look, I probably said more than I should have. A violation of the auntie-code and all that. I'll let you discuss with your boy when you get home."

"Good plan," I mumbled, resisting the urge to pump Tamara for more information. "Everything else is good?"

"Just the usual. Warhol broke his arm skateboarding, but that's fine. They were starting to miss us at the E.R. anyway. I do need to ask a favor, though."

"Anything."

"I've got a doctor's appointment on Tuesday. Can you watch the rugrats for me?"

"Absolutely," I agreed. "The annual fun-in-stirrups visit?"

Tamara paused.

"Nah. Actually, Howard ruined a perfectly good romantic moment in the shower a few weeks ago. Swore he felt a lump in my boob. So now I've gotta go get poked and prodded at Yale."

"Yale?" I felt a prickle along my skin. "Wouldn't you just go see your doctor first?"

Another pause.

"Yeah. I did that."

"Tam..."

"Oh, don't you fucking *Tam* me. You're as bad as

Howard. I've got lumpy tits. What can I say? That there's anything left of them at all after years of breastfeeding is a miracle. So I'll go get them abused some more, and put everybody's minds to rest, okay? Christ, I'd love to see them come up with a screening for testicular cancer that's half as brutal as what we go through with our squishy bits..."

I laughed in spite of myself.

Finn waved, nodding his head in the direction of the gate. Boarding for our flight had begun.

"I've gotta go," I told Tamara.

"You're flying commercial?" Tamara asked. "Isn't he a fucking billionaire or something? Why doesn't he have his own fucking plane?"

I laughed, thinking of the old pickup truck that was Finn's favorite mode of transportation, the battered stainless-steel watch and faded jeans that were his uniform.

"He's a very practical fucking billionaire," I smiled. "Though it's definitely first class all the way."

"Well, have a glass of Cristal or whatever the fuck they serve in first class for me, okay?"

"Okay!" I promised. "Can't wait to see you all, and no worries about Tuesday. I'll gladly be on kid-duty."

"Cool. And hey—if you have time on your layover, give Nate a call. He and Ian have some news."

"What?" I asked. "News? Can I not go away for any time at all without y'all changing everything up on me?"

"Sweetheart," Tamara laughed, "think about what happened the last time you took a vacation. This is mild, babycakes."

I laughed too, thinking back to the implosion of my life that had occurred during a single week at Ocean Manor in Watch Hill.

That I was even here, boarding a plane alongside a brilliant hunk of sexy man after we'd been on a paragliding escape to South America, well—Tam was right. That said brilliant hunk of sexy man would look at me as he did just then, with eyes full of the love I'd been waiting a lifetime to feel, was almost too much to bear. Finn put his hand lightly on my back as we started down the jetway.

Could too much love and gratitude be a shock to a system as long-neglected as mine?

If so, I was in danger.

And I was blissfully willing to accept the risk.

****

I dialed Nate on our layover, mistakenly making it a

FaceTime call.

"Hey, Nate!" I said when his face came into view. "I didn't mean to inflict FaceTime on you. I must look like hell after traveling all day."

"Shhh. Eve, keep it down," Nate whispered.

There was no mistaking his panic, both in his tone of voice and his expression. And Tamara's younger brother—whom I'd long considered my own adopted brother—was generally one of the most mellow people I knew.

Then I noticed his surroundings. He was crouched low amidst a sea of fabric: neatly-pressed slacks and shirts in various shades of Ian-grey to one side, the more colorful rainbow of Nate's usual Oxford shirts, sweater vests and khakis to the other side. Neat rows of footwear were visible above his head.

"Nate," I began, barely able to stifle a giggle, "are you in your closet?"

"It's not funny," he cautioned.

I laughed more fully.

"You're in the closet," I stated, "and it most definitely is funny. I mean, really. You're literally. In. The. Closet."

"Yeah, yeah, I get the joke," Nate hissed. "Ha, ha. Very funny. Except that it's not. Think about it, Eve. I am a grown man, and here I am hiding in my closet and whispering to you over FaceTime. This is the behavior of a man in distress. A man who *thought* he was chatting with a *friend*."

I forced a more serious expression onto my face.

"Honestly, Nate, I'm sorry. What the heck is going on? Are you under siege from terrorists? Or worse, the Alt-Right?"

I saw Nate crack the tiniest of smiles, then his face dissolved into dismay once again.

"They're evil," he whispered. "Pure evil. Not the sweet little cherubs we met with the social worker, no. Not the *'please-don't-let-us-age-out-of-the-system-without-a-family'* darlings. Eve, these are Rosemary's babies Ian and I have adopted. Two of them, with all the raging hormones and burgeoning body parts that come with pubescent girls. Sweet lord, you have no idea what we're dealing with here."

I relaxed a little bit. So Nate and Ian, gay men and brand-new adoptive fathers of thirteen year old twins, were inexperienced at dealing with teenaged girls. Big surprise there. Surely it wasn't as bad as he made it sound.

"Parenting stuff," I sighed. "I can help you out there. Or at least commiserate. I've got my hands full with the boys, I assure you. What's the issue? Go on. Shoot."

"What's the issue?" Nate exclaimed, his eyes bulging. Then he seemed to remember he was in hiding. His voice returned to a whisper. "What *isn't* the issue? They looked like normal, middle-American girls when we adopted them. We filled their closet with Kate Spade and Milly. Cute, fun stuff—you really should see. Anyway. Somehow they've emerged looking like Madonna had an orgy with Courtney Love and that moody vampire-bait chick."

Again, I tried to stifle a laugh.

"Kids like to push the limits with style," I said. I rolled my eyes. "I just heard Eli chose Lisbeth Salandar for his first girlfriend."

Nate shook his head vigorously.

"It's not just how they look. Within one week they were both evicted from school. It seems our little darlings teamed up to assault a classmate in the gym locker room—and they bypassed *Mean Girls* and went straight to *Carrie*." He gulped. "There were *bloody tampons* involved. And this isn't me using my faux-British 'bloody,' okay?"

All hint of a smile vanished from my face.

"Oh jeez, Nate. Okay, yes, those are seriously troubled girls," I agreed. I tried to find the silver lining. "But they need you. Really. They need you and Ian to give them some love and guidance and boundaries before it's too late. Think about it. Behavior like that is a cry for help. God knows what they've been through in their young lives. Clearly it hasn't been good. Look, I know how scary this must be, but you knew you weren't signing on for a walk in the park. You chose these girls as your daughters, and they chose you as their dads. There has to be a reason."

"Oh, there's a reason," Nate said, his voice low and self-loathing. "I'm an idiot. I'm a bleeding heart liberal who thinks I can fix everything that's wrong with the world with a kiss and a Band-Aid and a lollipop. I talked Ian into this, and the poor man looks like he's been shot at and hit. It's just too much."

"Well, you can't return them. This isn't a pair of cashmere socks we're talking about."

Nate inhaled deeply.

"Don't I know it. Ian and I had a long talk yesterday. He had a job offer in Connecticut that he'd turned down. He put in a call to the headhunter and let him know he's interested after all. And there's that house next door to Tam that's been on the market forever. It's ugly as sin, but for the right price, we could overhaul it. We put in an offer this morning."

I let out a squeal of joy.

"You're moving back?"

Nate waved his hands to calm me down.

"It's a whole lot of 'ifs' right now, but if things fall into place, yes. These girls need a fresh start. Lots of counseling. The kind of education they could get at Pinecroft. And dammit, Ian and I need help. We need family. It would be so good to have Tamara and Howard right next door, and you and your boys." Nate clapped his hand to his chest. "I've loved living in San Francisco, you know I have, but sometimes you just need to go home. And Eve, I've never needed home more than I do now."

I smiled at him gently.

"Well, Nate, you know I'll be thrilled to have you home. I've always been so grateful that Tamara let me borrow you, little bro."

In the background, I heard the sudden blare of loud music through speakers. Nate's gaze traveled to the closet door.

"I don't suppose I can hide out in here forever," he said. "It sounds like another storm is brewing. Love you, Eve. Now wish me strength."

"Strength!" I said, and I watched his worried face vanish from the screen.

Chapter **Two**

There was no way to gracefully transition from nearly two weeks of solitude in paradise with Finn to my life in Connecticut.

We arrived at Tamara and Howard's just as they were finishing dinner, and in short order, Finn and I were attacked by a swarm of small boys with sticky hands, filthy faces, and a relentless chorus: *What did you bring us, Auntie Eve?*

I parceled out treats, guilty of having bought them in the airport gift shop. My vacation with Finn had so removed me from reality, I'd forgotten this pack of wild boys and the way I'd conditioned them to expect little gifts with my every coming and going. They departed with their treasures as quickly as they'd descended.

"Wash your hands!" Tamara called out after them.

I caught Finn laughing. Those kids were as likely to wash their hands as he was to wear a skirt.

"A drink?" Howard offered from the far corner of the kitchen.

I realized Howard was, in fact, wearing a skirt. Though for him, this was only a slight departure from his typical gender-bending style. Howard's eyes, as usual, were ringed with more makeup than his wife wore, the lids drooping as though he'd already had quite a bit of the red wine in the bottle he swirled in our direction.

"I've got it, babe," Tamara winked, swatting Howard's rear end as she passed.

She pulled a beer from the fridge, popped it open and handed it to Finn. As she poured two glasses of Chardonnay and set them on the table, I noticed the tall, thin figure lurking in the doorway.

"Eli!" I called.

I went to my son and hugged him before he could protest. I marveled at his height. It was a strange thing, seeing the features I'd adored since his infancy set into this ever-growing, gangly frame. Could he have grown in the short time I was away, or was I just seeing him with fresh eyes?

"How are you?" I asked, leaning back but keeping his hands in mine. I pulled him close again and whispered, "I hear you have a girlfriend?"

"*Mom,*" Eli said, his voice a notch lower than I'd realized it could be.

"Oh, don't be silly. You can tell me about these things…"

"No, *Mom*…" Eli cautioned.

I felt the paws only a split-second before I felt the floor. And then there I was, flat on my back as my Leonberger 'puppy'—all 100 lbs. of him—slobbered joyfully on my face. I choked on the smell of dog breath.

"Well, I guess you're officially welcomed home now," Tamara joked. "Eli, help your mom, for chrissakes."

Eli smirked as he helped me up.

"This is why I'm a cat person," he said.

"A cat person with a girlfriend, I hear," I replied, unwilling to let it go.

"A cat person with a ton of homework," Eli said. He grabbed an apple from a bowl on the counter and made his escape. "Later! And welcome home!"

"You give birth to them, and they can't even give you five minutes," I sighed, sinking into a chair and taking a sip of wine.

"It could be worse," Tamara said. "He could be giving you holy hell. Did you talk to Nate?"

"Yes! He and Ian might be moving back East? I'm so excited! I mean, I'm sorry it's because they've adopted the bad seed times two, but you know..."

"I know," Tam laughed. "I thought he was exaggerating at first, but that incident at school..."

Finn squeezed my shoulder and gave me a wink. He cleared dishes from the table and brought them to Howard, who was singing as he filled the sink with soapy water.

"How are you feeling about Tuesday?" I asked Tamara.

"Shit, Eve, I should have told you I was going shopping. I knew you'd do this."

"Do what? Express concern for the health of my best friend? Yeah, I'm a bitch that way."

Tam raised her wine glass in one hand and extended the middle finger on her other. I stuck my tongue out at her.

"It'll be fine," she said at last. "Even if it *isn't* fine, you know? Don't they just cut that shit out and zap you with a few micro-waves these days? It's all good."

I took the hint, sipped my wine, and changed the subject.

"Nate told me he and Ian put an offer in on the split level next door. That's been on the market forever. He said it needs work. How bad is it?"

From the sink, Howard called over his shoulder.

"It's like 1969 and 1987 had a baby. And not in a good way."

Tam nodded in agreement.

"Faux brick linoleum in the kitchen. Orange shag carpeting everywhere else. And Howard's right: they removed the best 1960's design elements and replaced them with the worst of the '80's. Lots of shiny pink wallpaper. Popcorn ceilings caked with scented candle residue. That two gay men in the design business would even consider it tells you how desperate they are."

I winced.

"How would they do this?" I asked. "It doesn't sound like they could live there during the renovation."

"Not sure, really. We've got just one spare bedroom left here. I offered that the girls could take it, and Nate just about had a seizure, telling me I didn't know what I'd be getting into." Tamara smirked. "Like I'm new to this parenting rodeo."

As if on cue, a stampede overhead made its way down the stairs. Wielding an assortment of plastic baseball bats and Legos configured into weaponry, Howard and Tamara's boys chased each other through the kitchen.

"Hey!" Tam called. "We're nonviolent in this house, goddammit! Abandon your arms and get your little butts into the bathtub!"

She shook her head, drained her wine glass, then refilled it. Howard left the dishes to Finn and chased after the kids. I noticed his skirt made it difficult for him to run.

"Your husband is one of a kind," I grinned.

"Amen to that!" Tamara said, raising her glass.

I put a hand over my glass as she moved to refill it.

"I'd better not. I'm exhausted." I stood and called to Finn, "Need a hand over there?"

He laughed as he came over, wiping his hands on a dish towel.

"Oh, you and your timing! Did you watch to be sure I was finished?"

I stood and kissed him on the cheek.

"Moi?" I teased, wide-eyed.

He tickled me in response.

"Okay, lovebirds," Tamara said, rising from her chair. "I'd better go help Howard with the hooligans. Stay for another drink, if you like. I trust you'll take the beast with you when you go?"

She tipped her head at the puppy lounging on the floor, and Sammie raised his head as if he'd been called. I gave Tamara a hug and a kiss on the cheek.

"He's all mine. Thanks so much for looking after him—

and my human boys, too."

"One fur kid, one kid at boarding school, and one quiet guy with a girlfriend," Tam winked, returning my kiss. "It was a piece of cake. 'Night, sweetie. And welcome home."

I dashed upstairs and quickly gave Eli a goodnight hug and kiss. He actually reciprocated. I decided he might have missed me.

Finn wrapped his arm around my shoulder as we made our way to Nana's cottage. The night was cool, but the air smelled of spring. The stars above winked from behind wisps of cloud. Sammie bounded back and forth, hopefully exerting enough puppyish energy that he'd fall quickly to sleep once inside.

"I cannot thank you enough," I said to Finn as we reached the door. "That was an amazing trip. Beyond amazing, really."

That sly, sexy grin of his tugged at the corner of his mouth.

"That's it? You're giving me the boot?"

"Finn, I'm beat. Back to reality tomorrow. And don't you need to check on Oscar Wilde?"

"I'm sure the cat's been fine in Carla's care. I'm more concerned about how I'm supposed to sleep without you beside me, now that I've gotten used to it and all."

"That was nice, wasn't it?"

I melted into Finn's kiss. Truth be told, I didn't want to see him go, but the familiar surroundings had my mind clicking into gear. *There were so many things I needed to do!*

"It was very nice," he said. "So nice, actually, I was thinking maybe we should make a regular thing of it."

"What do you mean?" I asked before I could stop myself. I was pretty sure I knew where this was going, and I wasn't sure I wanted to have this conversation now.

"I mean, what if we did that every night, that sleepover business? I've got that big, empty house, and I know you like it here at Nana's cottage and all, but my place has room enough for the boys to each have their own space, and…" he trailed off as I put my finger to his lips.

Was I really silencing this beautiful man as he invited me—with baggage that included two teenage boys—to come live with him in Watch Hill?

"Finn, wow. That's a sweet idea, and a very generous offer, but…"

Finn winced dramatically.

"Ow. The dreaded 'but'…"

I nodded.

"But…can we just table the idea for now? Maybe talk about it another time? I'm not sure I'm ready in general, and

I'm definitely too tired to think about it right now."

He puckered up, twisting his mouth into a disappointed duckface. He was keeping it comical for my sake, I could tell. His eyes were humorless. Sad, even.

"Fair enough," he said, leaning in to kiss me on the forehead, then the nose. "Get some sleep, Eve. Enough that we can talk about this the next time I see your lovely face, because greedy as it may sound, I have to admit: the more time I spend with you, the more I want. Sleeping alone just ain't what it used to be."

With that much, I wholeheartedly agreed. I leaned in to kiss Finn again.

"True. And deal," I smiled as I sent him on his way.

And then, too tired to think about anything else, I dragged my spoiled, well-loved, and over-vacationed self off to bed.

****

And then, bright and early…

"*Ding dong, the bitch is dead.*"

Tamara dropped the newspaper onto my placemat next to my coffee cup. My eyes locked on the photo and my jaw dropped.

The obituary occupied a full page of the Newport paper.

Socialite and Philanthropist Kathryn Carter Wolcott, 89...

My hand went to my mouth.

"Kitty...is dead?" I shook my head, then scanned the page in search of some indication of how that woman of ice and steel had been felled.

"You're gonna want this," Tamara said, sliding her iPad in front of me.

It was open to an article in the more tabloid-esque local news feed. The headline screamed: *Trolley Terror in Tourist Town!*

There was no shortage of photos. I scrolled through image after image. Ambulances and police cars parked haphazardly on the cobblestone streets of Newport's waterfront district; Vineyard Vines-clad tourists leaning on each other, crying in clear distress; and then, the photo that explained it all to me: one of Newport's trolley-style buses planted nose-front in the side of a massive Mercedes. The solid German automobile had collapsed so fully around the front of the bus, it appeared to be made of tin foil. Feeling a bit nauseous, I enlarged the image. If I'd had any doubt as to ownership of the crushed vehicle, its vanity plate removed it.

KCW-1.

"Jesus," I whispered. I squinted, looking again at the minutae of the photo. "And is that...?"

"Kitty's Birkin bag lying in the middle of the street?" Tamara finished my query. "Yup. A fucking crime, that. And only in downtown Newport would a work of art like that be left lying there long enough for anyone to get a photo."

"Tam!" I scolded.

I tried to parse out the real story of what had happened from the sensational spin.

"She was getting out of the car," Tamara explained. "The trolley driver had a stroke or something. Have you ever noticed that all the drivers there are older than God? Anyway, he hit the gas, went through the crosswalk and plowed straight into Kitty's car just as her driver was helping her out."

"Oh no," I said. "Edwin..."

"The chauffeur? He's fine," Tamara assured me. "Missed him by a fraction of an inch. Pedestrians were all fine, too. Karma must've been gunning for Kitty."

I saw the tears hit the table before I realized I was shedding them.

"Oh man, don't. You are *not* crying over that evil bitch," Tamara said in quiet disbelief.

Oh god, I was, wasn't I?

Why on earth?

"Well, she was Eli and Max's grandmother," I sniffed defensively.

But it was more than that.

Kitty, with her ongoing demands for involvement in my sons' lives, was the last remaining tie to my former existence. She was Skip's mother. Haughty, vindictive, conniving—sure—but on some level I suppose I'd thought that made her immortal. Through all the incomprehensible changes over the past year, Kitty had been a constant. She was a thorn in my side, and I'd tried to wish her away, but I never really imagined she'd be gone. In fact, I imagined her outliving us all, her meanness a shield even against death. More than once, Tamara had joked that even the devil didn't want her. Kitty Wolcott's passing meant an era had ended, yes, but it meant something more than that.

It meant we all were vulnerable.

Tam reached over and squeezed my hand. I realized how quiet the house was. All the kids were at school. Even Tamara's little guys now had three days a week of Montessori. Howard was at his studio. The dog was outside, likely rolling in shit I'd have to bathe off him later. But the quiet. I could hear the grandfather clock ticking in the study down the hall. Time was truly marching on, change the only constant. I took a long sip of my coffee and found it had gone cold and bitter. I picked up a napkin and dried my eyes.

"I'll have to tell the boys," I said. Dread formed a hard ball in my belly. "Oh, Max. Poor Max. I should drive out to Morefield, tell him in person. But what about Eli? Should I pull him from school, maybe see if he wants to make the drive with me?"

"I'd let him finish out the day," Tamara suggested. "Tell him when you pick him up. You'll still have time to get to Max before dinner. Maybe let the headmaster know what's happened. Hell, he probably knows already."

Indeed. The Wolcotts had funneled so much money into that school over the years, their name graced multiple buildings. No doubt the headmaster—a man I'd found distasteful the few times we'd met—was already salivating in anticipation of the reading of Kitty's will.

"Good plan," I agreed, then I thought of something. "I was supposed to have dinner with Finn tonight. I'd better go fill him in."

I stood, kissed Tamara on the top of the head, and marveled again at the news.

"Want me to get someone else to watch the kiddos tomorrow?" Tamara asked.

"Nope," I called over my shoulder as I headed out the

door. "I'll deal with this today, then I imagine it will be a while before the service. I'm all yours tomorrow. I'll manage the wolf pack, you go get yourself a clean bill of health, okay?"

"Deal!"

I tapped my phone, dialing Finn as I made my way to the cottage. His low, sexy voice on the other end of the line always caught me slightly off-guard.

"Hey, sweetie."

"Hey," I began. "You haven't looked at the Newport paper today, have you? Because you will not believe what happened..."

****

I waited with the line of cars in front of Pinecroft's main building. At 2 p.m. exactly, students filed out the front door, then spilled into a loud, raucous crowd. Parents tooted car horns as kids pretended not to notice, laughing with their friends. I spotted Eli and was about to toot my own car horn as uselessly as all the others around me, but I stopped, my fingers hovering over the steering wheel.

A girl had moved in alongside him, and Eli—my quiet, antisocial son—slung his arm around her shoulder so easily, it seemed this happened all the time. She was taller than he, I noticed, as if she'd completed a growth spurt he'd yet to experience. And I saw why Tamara had joked that she was *The Girl With the Dragon Tattoo*; her appearance was dark and artfully cultivated, not entirely goth, but it might as well have been in this sea of preppy Connecticut kids. Her hair was jet back, a color I was certain came from a box, with severe bangs cut high above her neatly-penciled eyebrows. A trio of dark blue feathers cascaded from a hairpin somewhere above her temple. When her hand went to Eli's face (*dear Lord, she was touching my son!*), I saw that her short, blunt fingernails were painted a similar dark blue, with just enough sparkle to catch the light. I felt my jaw drop as the girl kissed my boy, but just as I wondered if I should look away, she took her lips (lightly berry-pink) off my child and moved away, headed for a car somewhere further back in the line.

Eli watched her go, then looked around as if awakening to his surroundings. He found my car, waved, and made his way over.

"Hey there," I said as he slid into the passenger seat.

"Hey."

"So... Um... Is that the girlfriend?"

Eli's eyes darted at me, but he kept his head carefully facing forward.

"Girlfriend?"

"Yeah. You know. Isn't that what it's still called? I mean, she put her lips on your face. I assume there's some sort of special relationship there."

Eli laughed.

"Yeah. I guess so. That's Freya."

"And…" I prompted.

"And what?"

" *'That's Freya'*," I quoted. "Tell me more."

"What's to tell?"

"Oh Eli, keep it up and I'm going to have you Google 'infanticide' before I commit it."

Again, he laughed. He poked earbuds into his ears, and I reached over—gently, wordlessly—and pulled them out. He gave a heavy sigh.

"I guess she's my girlfriend. She's a year older, but we're in photography together. She runs track and cross country, too, but we only see the girls' team on the bus."

Unbidden, an image of my son and this Freya-person making out at the back of a school bus came to me. I blinked it away.

"Is she nice?" I asked.

"No, Mom. She's a total jerk. That's why I'm into her."

It was my turn to laugh. I resisted the urge to say I was

afraid I might've passed a taste for jerks down to him. After all, in my life, it was Eli's father who'd been the jerk.

"Got it," I said. "Well, bring her over sometime. I want to meet this girl who kisses my son in front of the entire dismissal line at Pinecroft."

I glanced over at Eli in time to see his face flush red.

Mom-goal achieved.

"Um, okay. She'd probably like that. She doesn't know anyone here yet. Her family just moved here."

"Oh. From where?"

"Somewhere in Massachusetts. Out in the Berkshires."

"Where I went to college," I commented.

"Yeah," Eli smiled, popping the earbuds back in. "There are a lot of colleges out there."

I nodded, flipping the directional and turning.

"Hey—where are we going?" Eli asked as we merged onto the highway instead of heading home.

The brief feeling of levity our conversation had offered abandoned me. How to say this?

"We're going to Max's school," I said. There was a long pause in which I felt his questioning gaze on me. "Eli, I'm so sorry to have to tell you this, but your grandmother passed away."

Long pause.

Long, long pause.

"Oh," he said at last. "Well. She was, like, ancient, right?"

I bit my tongue.

"Um, she was...*older*," I conceded.

"How'd she die?"

I tried to put the news feed images out of my mind: the crushed Mercedes, Kitty's vanity plate, her handbag on the cobblestone.

"It was an accident. A car accident."

"Oh man," Eli said. "Doesn't Edwin always drive her? Is he okay?"

It occurred to me that this was the first note of genuine concern that had entered my son's voice. He had a much closer relationship with his grandmother's chauffeur, I realized, than with the Ice Queen herself.

"Edwin's fine," I assured him. "He was very lucky."

"Cool. Oh man," Eli said again, deeper concern seeping into his voice. "Max."

I nodded.

"He was very close to your grandmother. That's why we're going to Morefield in person."

"Good call, Mom," Eli affirmed.

He adjusted his ear buds, sank down in his seat, and

gazed out the window as he turned on his music. I could hear the tinny notes from the driver's seat, and thought of cautioning him once again about damaging his hearing. But I didn't. He had that knowledge already. Offering it again and again would be nagging, for certain.

So I just drove, awash in affection for the long-legged young man in the seat beside me, even as the feeling of dread grew with every mile that brought us closer to my other boy, Max, and the painful truth I would have to deliver.

****

"What are you doing here?" Max spat.

He'd removed his tie, and the unbuttoned collar of his Oxford shirt flapped open around the neck of his Morefield blazer. His blonde curls were askew, and I was surprised by the gut feeling that he looked much, much older already since I'd last seen him, only weeks ago. He looked older—and he looked increasingly like Skip. Only Skip. As if my genetic material were being edged out by the day.

"I need to talk to you," I said.

I nodded my head in the direction of the empty office the headmaster had made available to us. Accommodating, that man. I could almost see the dollar signs in his eyes when he offered his condolences. No doubt he had plans for a new building already in the works.

Max planted his feet firmly where he stood. An arch of granite curved high above him, and a heavy oak door stood ajar just beyond, as if offering escape. I realized Max's eyes were red-rimmed and bloodshot.

"I already know," he said. "It's all over the news. Everyone knows. We had a moment of silence earlier. Do you know how much Gramma did for this school?"

I felt as though I'd been slapped. Here it was, another maternal failure. He'd learned of his grandmother's death on the news, and now he was lecturing me on her significance to Morefield as if I were a stranger. Was there nothing I could do right in Max's eyes?

"Max, sweetheart, I am so sorry."

I moved in to hug him and he backed away. I felt tears threatening to spring to my eyes, and I forced them back. If anyone would know they were tears of self-pity, not tears of grief, it would be Max, and he would hold it against me indefinitely. I looked at the man-child before me and realized I no longer needed to tilt my head in order to make eye contact. He'd grown, and he'd be my height in no time at all now.

"Max, grief is hard. You don't have to go it alone.

That's why you have family. That's why we're here."

I paused, glancing over my shoulder at Eli, who'd folded himself onto a bench at the far side of the corridor. His earbuds remained solidly in place, and his face was aglow with light from the screen of his iPhone. His posture said he'd rather be anywhere but here. The brotherly bond I'd envisioned for my boys had never materialized, yet I held out hope.

"Max," I continued, "you've lost so much this year. We all have." I ignored his wry snort and went on. "Come on. Let's go out to dinner. We can share some good memories about Gramma."

At this, Max let out a guffaw. It echoed in the stone all around.

"Give it up," he said. "You hated her. I bet it made your day to hear she's gone."

"That's not true," I interrupted, but I could feel my face going crimson with shame. The worst of me went transparent before my second son.

"It is," he insisted. "And you know what? I don't care. It doesn't matter. She hated you, too. So why don't you two go on back to your world, and leave me in mine. I'm gonna be late for dinner, and I've got an exam to study for."

Max glowered at both me and Eli. I felt nauseous.

"The headmaster said you could come home," I said

quietly. "You can take the exam later. Let's at least go have dinner, and you can see how you feel about it."

"I know how I feel about it, thanks, and I'll stay right here." Max folded his arms across his chest, and I flashed briefly to his petulance as a toddler. "I'm sorry you wasted the drive, but I'm all set."

"The funeral…" I began.

"Won't be for another week or so," Max cut in. "I talked to Uncle Shep. He'll pick me up on his way from Mattapoisett. I can stay with him at Gramma's house, then he'll bring me back."

I was dumbstruck. My boy, barely thirteen, had made all the plans necessary to get himself to his grandmother's funeral. That he'd allied himself with one of Skip's brothers was only a minor surprise. Max fit so well with the Wolcott clan.

"Well, then." I said.

My hands flapped awkwardly at my sides.

"Well, then," Max echoed. "I told you—I'm all set, you see?"

And then he did something that sent chills down my spine.

He stepped forward, placed his hands on my upper arms with surprising firmness, and lightly kissed my cheek. He turned me around, deliberately aiming me at the door, but not before I caught sight of his face. His eyes were clear and steely, as if he'd willed the redness away. Any trace of emotion had vanished from his face. His expression was eerily placid. It took me in an instant back to Skip's father's passing—the way Skip had fallen apart, then composed himself with alarming speed. I looked at my son's face, and all I could see was my late husband.

"Drive safely, Mother," Max said, and I was dismissed.

I stood there, frozen between Eli and the heavy oak door with its wrought iron hinges aimed like daggers at the way out. I listened to the receding click of Max's penny loafers on the stone floor as he vanished in the opposite direction. Eli rose, keeping his eyes carefully focused on his phone, and put a hand gently to my elbow. He steered me out of the building and back to the car, where we sat in silence for several moments before I turned the key.

Even then, it was several more minutes more before I could drive. I summoned every meditation technique I'd ever learned, trying to steady myself and prevent the flood of tears that felt ready to burst forth. My mantra was so elementary, it was painful:

Breathe.

Breathe.

Breathe.

"Mom?" Eli said quietly. "Are you okay?"

I patted his hand and bit my lip.

"I'm okay, Eli," I said at last. "And I absolutely love that you asked."

Eli shrugged.

"What can I say? I'm not an asshole."

I laughed loudly, gratefully. His use of the expletive sailed right past my Mom-radar, it was so perfect.

"Oh, Eli—indeed you are not!"

I started the car and quickly got us off the Morefield campus. As we merged back onto the highway, headed for home, I glanced over at Eli. It was dark out now. Shadows from outside passed over his face, and the glow of his phone illuminated his features from below. I felt a rush of affection I could barely contain.

I also felt guilty, because wasn't a mother supposed to love her children equally? And I loved Max—of course I loved Max—but it felt increasingly like the same twisted, elusive sort of love I'd felt for his father, a thing I would forever chase and never quite catch.

But Eli.

My love for Eli felt like something else altogether. An affinity between kindred spirits, maybe. The kind of thing where understanding was tacit and empathy a given.

"That Freya," I said quietly, my eyes on the road. "I hope she appreciates what she's got in you."

Eli said nothing, but I caught his sideways glance, and the little smile that flickered at the corner of his mouth.

Chapter **Three**

I dropped Eli at the main house without going inside, then continued down the drive to the cottage. I was only slightly surprised to see Finn's truck parked out front.

"I heard there was a dog here in need of walking and feeding and petting," he said, taking my jacket and purse and hanging them on the coat rack. "I also thought you might need at least one of those things tonight, too."

I smiled and kissed his cheek.

And then I fell apart.

Truly.

I collapsed into a blubbering mass of jelly.

"Man, I really do it for you, don't I?" Finn joked when

the worst of my sobbing had subsided.

I laughed, and to my horror, I felt a giant glob of snot escape a nostril. Finn grabbed a Kleenex and wiped my nose as if I were a child.

"You know," he teased, "when I said I enjoyed getting your juices flowing, I probably should have been more specific."

I laughed again and punched his arm.

God, that arm!

Rock solid with muscle.

And yeah, now juices more sexy than snot were flowing.

Finn kissed me, then put his nose to mine.

"I love you, Eve. I'm sorry you had such a shitty time of it tonight." He paused and winked. "You know, I don't usually beat up kids, but if you need me to open a can of whoopass on that little prep school punk of yours…"

We both laughed then. I realized I loved Finn's warped sense of humor as much as his many other wonderful attributes.

In short order, we found ourselves kissing.

Somehow we rolled from the sofa onto the floor. Mistaking this for an invitation to play, the dog bounded up from his corner, tail wagging, and began licking our faces.

"Hey, buddy!" Finn laughed, pushing him off. "Get back on your dog bed! I'm not into that sort of thing."

Finn stood and pulled me up. Sammie, realizing his

enthusiasm was meeting with an obstacle, retreated to his dog bed with a sigh. I took Finn by the hand and pulled him into the bedroom.

I fell back onto the bed, and he sank to his knees in front of me.

His hands, so large and strong, pushed my dress up to my waist. I felt his lips on my thighs, his teeth at my panties. Then he leaned back, unzipping my boots and setting them neatly to the side. His tongue grazed the bands of my thigh-high stockings, then he began rolling them down my legs with a slowness that raised goosebumps on my skin. He drew his lips lightly back up my bare legs, over the thin fabric of my panties. All thought escaped me, likely because all blood had rushed from my brain, fueling the throbbing between my legs. I felt his tongue there at the innermost crease of my thigh, teasing, running along the edge of my panties. My back arched, and I looked down just in time to catch him grinning.

Finn loved to tease me.

I loved it, too.

How long did it take for him to finally remove my panties?

Only forever.

I came once, hard, before he even pulled that little bit of fabric from me, and then again only moments after he was inside me. I ran my hands across his broad shoulders and down his muscled back, marveled at the way a slight tilt this way or that could increase pleasure I thought was already exquisite.

We did this so often—how was it possible that it felt so damn good every time?

I felt his body rock, shudder, pulse with his orgasm. He leaned into me, all that was tense in him going deliciously, warmly slack. His head bent into the crook of my arm, and then he raised it, and there it was once again: that unflinching gaze of his.

My eyes met his, and I smiled.

"I love you, Eve," he said.

I could barely breathe.

"I love you, Finn," I whispered.

The words rattled around in my brain. They filled my heart. Had I ever meant them for anyone else in the same way I meant them for Finn? And how could that be? How could love be something so varied and nuanced that it was never the same thing between one pair of people as it was between another?

"Where are those thoughts of yours taking you?" Finn mused, kissing me gently.

His smile crinkled the lines around his eyes and again, my affection for him swelled.

"Good places," I said sincerely. "Very, very good

places."

****

By noon the next day, it seemed impossible I'd ever inhabited such a space of tranquility and bliss.

I loved Tamara's boys (truly, I did) but dear lord, had wilder creatures ever existed in the history of humankind? By the time Tam walked in the door from her doctor's appointment, I was toast.

"That bad, huh?" she queried with a grin as she set her purse down in the hallway.

I realized my expression had given me away.

"Nah, not all. Nothing therapy won't fix," I teased.

"It's quiet now. Should I be concerned? Dragging the lake, maybe?"

I averted my eyes, leading the way into the kitchen.

"I caved," I admitted, then shoved a sandwich in front of Tam to distract her. "They're playing a game on the computer."

Tamara laughed. She sat down and spoke through her first bite of lunch.

"The modern world was bound to get them eventually, I suppose."

I sat across from her and asked, "So?"

"So. Now we wait."

"How long? This isn't one of those 'No news is good news' deals, is it? That drives me crazy."

"Luckily, they said I'll hear something one way or the other by the end of next week. I gotta tell you, though—have you ever had your boob biopsied?"

I shook my head.

"I don't recommend it," she said tersely. "Fucking medieval."

I truly couldn't imagine.

"Hey!" she said as if struck by a sudden thought. "Have you talked to Nate?"

I shook my head.

"I saw I missed a call from him this morning, actually, but I, ah, didn't quite have a moment to call him back."

Tamara laughed as she took another bite of her sandwich.

"I can imagine. Well, listen. I talked to him on the drive home, and they accepted their offer on the place next door. It's official: Nate and Ian are moving in next week!"

"Sweet! Wait. Next week? What about renovations? Are they really going to live there while they do all the work it needs? Because I can see Ian having a nervous breakdown over that. He's kind of OCD, you know?"

"Kind of?" Tam winked. "Nate said something about a motor home Ian's parents are going to lend them so they can stay on-site while the work is done."

I couldn't help but laugh.

"Okay, wait—I can't decide which idea I find more bizarre: Nate and Ian in a motor home, or Ian having parents."

Tamara laughed with me.

"Right? I mean, I always figured Ian sprang in adult form from some Danish modern god's head. But apparently, he was actually born as an infant. To people who own a fast food chain and live in Florida, no less."

"You're joking."

Tamara held up her fingers.

"Scout's honor. Do you think I could make that shit up?"

Truly, I did not.

"You know," she elaborated. "The Chicken King? Those horrible commercials? *More cluck-cluck-cluck...*"

"*For your buck-buck-buck!*" I finished, my eyes widening in horror.

Tam nodded.

"That's Ian's dad."

"*No!*"

"Yes!" she laughed. "That's their chain, and Ian's father

is The Chicken King himself."

"No," I said again. "But Ian's so...*dignified.* And isn't he vegan?"

"That he is. Probably one more reason to avoid eating at The Chicken King. When the heir to the throne won't touch the stuff, well…"

"Oh jeez," I said, realization dawning. "Ian's the Chicken Prince."

"Call him that when he gets here," Tamara joked. "I bet we'd finally see that quiet, dignified man lose his shit."

"Momma!" a small voice cried from the doorway, and Reed, Tamara's youngest, dashed over and climbed onto her lap. "Chicken?"

"No baby," she said, licking her thumb and wiping a crust of something from the corner of his mouth. "No chicken in this house. 'Cept maybe you."

She tickled Reed and he writhed, giggling.

I felt a twinge, remembering when my boys had been that age. There was something nice about being able to scoop them up and kiss and tickle them at will. But then again, there was also something nice about the drive home with Eli the night before, the way he'd expressed concern for me. It almost made up for the chasm between me and Max.

Almost.

"Hey, Tam, if you're all set here, I'm going to head back to the cottage. I've actually got an interview tomorrow at the animal rescue, so I want to get ready. And get this: Eli's bringing Freya home with him after school."

"Freya," Tamara said slowly. "You mean Ms. Salandar?"

"Yup."

"Excellent! Don't let her get away without meeting me."

"You got it," I said. "And let me know as soon as you hear from your doctor."

"End of next week," Tamara reminded me.

"Right," I said.

"And Eve," Tam called as I headed out the door, "don't make yourself crazy over the job. You've basically asked them to demote you at a place of employment where you're loved. You do realize it's a done deal, right?"

"Don't say that!" I called back. "You'll jinx me! If there's one thing I've learned in the past year, it's that nothing's a given. Love you!"

"Love you more!"

****

It was the kind of New England spring day that made it seem possible that summer might eventually arrive. April showers had yet to bring May flowers—really, if anything, May had been rainier so far than the preceding month—but this day was dry and clear, and the air smelled of damp earth and fresh grass. I threw the ball for Sammie so he'd get a workout that exceeded the distance between the main house and the cottage. He bounded back and forth in the game of fetch, expending twice as much energy as was necessary with each step. My plan worked. By the time we got home, he drank deeply from his water dish, then settled into his dog bed. I sat down with my laptop and triple-checked my resume.

It was sort of a joke. All volunteer work for the better part of the past two decades. And here I was applying for a job that would barely pay a living wage and was, indeed, a demotion from my current position. Was I shooting myself in the foot? I couldn't live in Nana's cottage forever, but I couldn't bear to think too far ahead, either. I had goals, but frankly, since Skip died and left us broke, I hadn't the faintest idea how to begin achieving them. I'd been working at the local animal rescue for a few months now, but I figured out fairly quickly that the position of volunteer coordinator was not for me. Sure, it was what I was best-qualified for, given my years as Skip's wife. I'd followed the Wolcott tradition and been a sort of professional volunteer. I did my current job well, but I hated it. The week the assistant shelter manager was out sick and I found myself cleaning cages and walking dogs was the best week I'd had. I realized I preferred dealing with animals to dealing with people. Dogs never complained that you scheduled them to work with someone they disliked. Cats never signed up for a shift, then bailed. Even cleaning up their messes felt meditative, while cleaning up human messes was a minefield of personality issues and complications.

I went to the bedroom and removed a cigar box from the bottom drawer of the bedside table. I sifted through the clippings and sketches it contained. Many were so old, they predated my marriage to Skip, but when I'd found this treasure in the course of my move, I'd begun adding to it again. Farmland, animals, tiny houses, solar panels, gardens overflowing with fresh produce. It was funny, really. I remembered sitting in my cramped apartment in Boston, back in my law school days, snipping some of these images out of *Better Homes and Gardens* magazine and imagining my law career would afford me a country home, a sort of gentlewoman's farm where I could rescue abandoned dogs, feral cats, horses ready to be put out to pasture. I even envisioned writing, maybe turning my courtroom experiences into fiction in the vein of Scott

Turow. I'd always loved telling stories.

Considering my dreams now felt odd. There'd been no law career after all, just a brief stint with a small firm in Providence that ended before Eli's birth. And while Skip and I had the Jamestown home, with its lawns rolling down to the ocean and my gardens gracing every corner, it wasn't the farm of my youthful dreams. For one key thing, Skip was not a fan of animals. He'd conceded that a dog might be good for the boys, but he'd never warmed up to Sally, and inviting more critters into our world was just not an option. I'd lost it once, drunkenly yelling at Skip that he was never home, so why the hell did he even care? But then I'd let it go, apologizing in the sobering light of morning and shelving my small-farm plans.

Childhood was for crazy dreams.

Adulthood was all about reality.

But reality could be funny. Here I was: forty, widowed, broke, and working at an animal rescue. When the assistant shelter manager gave her notice, I approached the director apprehensively. I knew he loved the job I'd been doing as volunteer coordinator, and predictably, he was surprised that I'd opt for a more menial hands-on position. But he took my resume and said he'd run it by the board. And now, tomorrow, I'd have my official interview.

I put the clippings back into the box, and said a little

prayer as I fastened the lid.

Chapter **Four**

Three-thirty in the afternoon.

The sun remained higher in the sky than usual, hinting at the lengthening days, and I noted the fuzz of yellow-green on the underbrush lining the road.

I also noted just how surreal a situation I'd once again found myself in.

My running shoes hit the pavement in synch with Finn's footfalls. That I could keep pace with him was a testament to his restraint; I knew he could outrun me in a heartbeat.

And there, just far enough ahead that we couldn't make out the particulars of their conversation, Eli and Freya ran side-by-side. They too could have left me in the dust, or could have just opted out of a run altogether, given that they already had so few days off from track, but here we were. Freya's jet black hair bobbed in a ponytail, and she reached out and tapped Eli's elbow, saying something that made them both laugh. I felt a sudden, almost overwhelming, surge of affection for this strange girl. I mean, *she made Eli laugh.* I looked over at Finn and smiled.

"I know, I know," he said, grinning back at me. "You love her right now. But if she hurts your boy, you'll hunt her down and kill her."

I laughed loudly enough that the young pair in front of us turned. I smiled and waved at them.

"Exactly," I said to Finn.

Sammie trotted along obediently at Finn's side. The trick of running to heel (as opposed to, say, darting in front of the runner and sending her flying) was one he'd mastered for Finn but was still working on with me. It didn't seem to matter that I was the one who filled his food dish every morning and evening; Sammie had clearly bonded with Finn before being turned over to my care. Finn was his pack leader. Well, unless Oscar Wilde was present. That cat bossed Sammie around to a degree that was hysterical.

We rounded the bend, passing one of the small farms I always admired. Like so many of the properties in the area, it appeared to be the pet project of someone who escaped the big city on weekends. Only the driveway of the little groundskeeper's cottage was occupied on a daily basis, though cars with New York plates lined the drive on the days when light spilled out of the windows of the main house. Out near the barn, there were a couple of alpacas, a couple of goats, and a dozen or so of the most beautiful and variously-colored chickens I'd ever seen, all wandering in happy oblivion through their beautiful yard. The raised beds that were still covered in straw now would soon be overflowing with heirloom vegetables. In late summer, there would be pops of color from flowers here and there, and the most amazing display of sunflowers in the fields behind the barn.

"That's all I need," I said jokingly to Finn as we ran past. "Just a little place like that. A few acres. Price tag ever-so-slightly over a million bucks. You know."

I realized as soon as the words were out of my mouth that I was joking with a man who could buy a place like that without batting a single one of his knee-weakening eyelashes. I felt suddenly embarrassed. I forgot sometimes how thoroughly broke I was, and how damn filthy rich he was. And then, when I remembered, I wished I could forget again. The imbalance between us seemed destined to cause trouble eventually.

"Well, now I know what to get you for your birthday,"

Finn said, and the teasing tone of his voice allowed me to exhale.

We came into the home stretch, and I noticed the 'Under Contract' sign on the house that would soon belong to Nate and Ian. For the first time, I really looked at it. Structurally, it had nice lines, clean and mid-century modern. I imagined it must have been beautiful when it was first built, and I knew Nate and Ian would restore it to its former glory. *But oh, did they have their work cut out for them.* Everything about the property spoke of neglect, from the overgrown gardens to the chipped paint and bits of roof flapping in the breeze.

"Mom, is that where Nate and Ian are gonna live?" Eli called over his shoulder.

"Yup!" I called, and I watched him tuck back into conversation with Freya. The one word I caught was, 'cool,' so I imagined they either saw potential, or Eli was just glad to know his honorary uncles would soon be neighbors.

"They've adopted two teenage girls?" Finn commented. "I may need to talk with Nate and Ian. I chatted with Molly last night, and she wants to come out here for college. I told her sure, but I've gotta be honest—I have no idea how to be an instant parent to a teenage girl."

"Well, Nate and Ian may not exactly be the folks to talk to, unless you're just looking to commiserate. It sounds like they're at their wits' end. But I do love the idea of you spending

62

more time with your daughter, you know."

"I thought you might," Finn replied. "One more battle won in the war to domesticate me, eh? But before I get too settled, how would you feel about going on another paragliding adventure? There's a fly-in next week that might be fun."

"Next week?" I asked, genuinely surprised. "We just got back from a trip. I've got that job interview tomorrow, and then they might actually expect me to work." I leaned over and elbowed him as we took the turn onto Tamara and Howard's driveway. "You remember that thing called work, right? Some of us have to do it to get by."

Finn laughed.

"Ha! How quickly you've become one of the teeming masses!"

I stuck my tongue out at him. Up ahead, Eli and Freya broke into a home-stretch sprint. I winked at Finn and took off after them.

Mere seconds later, Sammie came barreling past me, nearly knocking me over. In short order, Finn drew up alongside me, giving my rear end a light whack with the leash he'd unfastened from the dog.

"Hey!" I cried, laughing.

Finn passed me and caught up with Eli. The two headed into the house for water, Sammie trailing behind. I decided to do the mom-thing and catch Freya. I sidled up to the porch, where she was gracefully stretching. I tried to coolly lean into a pigeon pose, and instead ended up awkwardly pretzeled on the lawn before her. Freya raised an eyebrow at me.

"So," I said once I caught my breath. "Eli tells me you moved here from the Berkshires?"   "Mmmhmmm."

Oh goody. She was as talkative as my own kids. This would be as much fun as a root canal.

"Um, whereabouts, exactly? I went to school out there. So did Tamara. Mount Holyoke."

"Funny," she said, looking at me. She wiped sweat from her face, and mascara smudged across her cheeks. "My mom went to Mount Holyoke, too. And we didn't live far from there. Over in North Adams. My mom ran the volunteer program at the museum there."

"Huh. I wonder if I know your mom. What year was she at Mount Holyoke?"

Freya laughed.

"I dunno. Middle Ages?" she paused, then, looking stricken by a sudden thought. "I mean, I think she's a lot older than you. Like, a *lot*."

I smiled gently. Good save.

"How'd you end up here?"

"My dad's marrying his secretary. I mean, once he's no

longer married to my mom." Again, the pause, the stricken look. She fiddled with the bullring in her nose. "But that's way, way TMI, isn't it?"

I shook my head.

"Nah. I'm sorry. For you and for your mom. That's a tough thing to go through."

"Yeah. Whatever. So, my mom got this job offer here, at the nautical museum? And then we got out here and it fell through. So now she's shitting a brick." Freya's eyes went wide again. "Sorry. You must think I'm an asshole. Oh jeez. And now I've said asshole. Like, twice."

"I think you fit in perfectly here," a voice said from the doorway.

Tamara came out with two glasses of water and handed one to each of us. She sat on the step.

"Sorry I didn't join you on your run, but I have this idea that if a person is running, something should be fucking chasing her."

Freya and I both laughed. Finn and Eli came out of the house, and Sammie bounded after, bypassing the porch steps in favor of an impressive leap over the shrubbery. Two of Tamara's boys followed suit.

"Oh crap," Freya said as Eli sat down beside her. "My mom. She's early."

All eyes went to the Volvo station wagon that pulled up in front of the house. A petite woman in a pink tennis sweater and pearl earrings emerged. As she neared the porch, she worked a thin smile onto her face.

"I'm Heidi," she began, looking from me to Tamara as if trying to decide which of us she should be addressing.

As I stood, wishing I weren't so sweaty and disheveled, Tamara pushed suddenly in front of me.

"Holy fuck, you sure are!" she cried, embracing the startled woman. "Heidi fucking Macomber! No fucking way!"

My hand went to my mouth. I moved in for a closer look, but there was no doubt. It was Heidi Macomber, our R.A. from our Mount Holyoke days. She'd run our dorm with military efficiency, and everything was so fully her way or the highway, it had become a joke among the rest of us. Her name became code for perfectionism and micromanagement. Now, here she was, standing in Tamara's driveway so many miles from Hadley, Massachusetts, and a virtual lifetime later. Her daughter was dating my son. As coincidences went, this was a weird one.

"Oh my god," I breathed, going over to join in the hug.

"Tamara? Eve?" Heidi stammered. "I can't... I just..."

"I know!" Tam cried. "Fucking crazy, right?"

I disentangled from the embrace and glanced over at

Finn, Eli and Freya, who were trying to make sense of it all.

"You guys, like, know each other?" Eli asked.

Heidi laughed.

"We were in the same college class," she said.

"Well, actually, you were two years ahead of us," Tamara began, but Heidi cut her off with a glance. *The* glance. She still had it.

"Wow," Freya said. "Just... Wow."

I winked at her as we led her mother into the house.

"Life is weird," I said. "And it's a small, small world."

****

Over dinner, we learned the general story of how Heidi's life had gone—and then gone and unraveled—since college. There were some parallels between her story and mine that made a tendril of sympathy reach out from me to her. It sounded as though her soon-to-be-ex husband and Skip were cut from the same cloth.

Once dishes were cleared and kids left the table, the atmosphere shifted. Howard began the process of baths and bedtime with the kids, Finn excused himself to go plan another paragliding escape, and Eli and Freya dug into their homework in the study, since it seemed clear we'd be a while.

And we were.

We killed two bottles of wine. It was shameful enough on a Tuesday, but worse once Tamara and I realized Heidi had done the bulk of the drinking, and was unraveling.

"I just don't understand," she wept. "I did *everything* for that man. Everything! But they're all the same. They're all great, big dummies who follow that dumb-stick of theirs through life!"

Considering my own experience, it would have been tough to argue against her point, but given Heidi's condition, commentary of any kind seemed unwise. I bit my lip as she continued to vent drunkenly, while Tamara silently marveled at Heidi's benign choice of expletives, mouthing so only I could see: *Dummies? Dumb-stick?*

At some point, Heidi stood, swaying, and reached for the keys to her Volvo.

"Uh-uh," Tamara said, deftly scooping them from Heidi's manicured fingertips. "Nobody's going anywhere tonight. We've all been drinking, and we're all staying put."

"But I'm fine," Heidi protested. "And Freya has school tomorrow…"

"At the same school Eli attends," I said. "I'll drive them both in."   "She's very particular about her wardrobe,"

Heidi mumbled.

"I've got no end of black shit in my closet," Tamara countered. "And my sense of style is completely inappropriate for my age. The kid'll be fine."

"But I need to be home. I need to find a job," Heidi whined.

The lightbulb went on in my head.

"I have an idea about that," I told her. I gave her a glass of water. "Drink this, get some sleep, and we'll talk in the morning. I think I have just the thing for you."

Tamara raised an eyebrow at me, and I gave her the 'okay' sign.

"Alrighty, then—I think it's all settled," Tamara said with finality. "Heidi, come with me and let's make up the sofa in the study for you. Eve, can you set Freya up on your sofa so we don't have to worry about any teenage body parts going bump in the night?"

I winced.

"Absolutely."

And so it was that I ended up with Lisbeth Salandar—my weird son's weirder girlfriend—sleeping on my sofa while Sammie curled up happily on the floor beside her. I learned that the bullring was indeed a clip-on, and that with a freshly-washed face, she looked about ten years old. I wondered if she and Eli talked with each other about their respective family crises, if they felt kinship and support in common disaster. I hoped so. While part of me was still getting used to the idea of Eli having a girlfriend, another part felt distinct fondness beginning to grow for the girl he'd chosen.

In the morning, Freya and I walked together up to Tamara's house for breakfast. Surprisingly, Heidi looked none the worse for wear, and she expertly turned the experience into a drunk-driving lesson for her daughter. There was no mention of the fact that she'd been ready to take both of them out on the road the previous night. I was disturbed and impressed in equal measure. Heidi was still always right.

After breakfast, Tam and I traded charges. She led Freya upstairs to her closet, while I took Heidi to the cottage and tried to find something petite and preppy enough for her to wear. She wrinkled her nose at my wardrobe while I explained my plan: I would bring her with me to my interview at the animal rescue league, and recommend her to the board as my replacement in the volunteer coordinator position.

"I don't understand," she said. "You want me to take your administrative job so you can shovel poo? Why on earth?"

"Because," I began, attempting to explain, "as it turns out, I prefer shoveling poo to managing people."

"Are they horrible people?" Heidi asked suspiciously.

I laughed.

"No! They're lovely people, really. They're volunteers at an animal shelter—how horrible could they be? They're doing a good thing for the community. But I still like dogs and cats better."

Heidi continued to regard me quizzically, as if I were trying to put one over on her.

"Look," I said. "Just come with me and meet the board. Who knows? Maybe they won't even like you. But give it a shot, and let's see. And hey—if you want to run home to change, you've got time. I'll drive Eli and Freya to school, then meet you back here."

It took Heidi a moment to reply. I wondered if she was stuck on the incomprehensible notion that the board might not like her.

"Fine," she said at last. "It will give me an opportunity to print out my resume, too."

"Good!" I handed her a bottle of Visene. "A little bit of this wouldn't hurt, either. I'll see you back here in an hour."

"An hour!" she cried. "My hair takes…"

"An hour," I said firmly. "I know you can meet deadlines, Heidi. Shake that tiny little ass of yours."

She looked as though I'd slapped her, but she took the bottle of Visene and left with a barely-audible, "Hmmpf!"

****

The board loved Heidi.

Of course.

In our college days, there'd been no panel of authority figures she couldn't charm, and her skill remained intact.

And, as it turned out, they all agreed I'd be a good fit for shoveling shit. I wondered briefly if this might be the legacy of a Wolcott marriage. After a fair amount of joking about how this was the first time any of them had seen a job candidate arrive at an interview with her replacement in tow, the board offered positions to both me and Heidi. We went out for brunch in the village to celebrate.

It was warm enough that we sat out on a deck overlooking the harbor. I could feel the freckles rising on my skin in the late-morning sun. There were more boats in the water now, I noticed, than there'd been just a few weeks earlier, and a line of ducklings following their mother streamed across the glassy surface close to shore.

I watched Heidi down two Bloody Marys in impressively rapid succession, while her omelette remained largely untouched.

"Have you found a counselor locally?" I asked, dispensing with tact entirely. "Mine is wonderful, if you need a name."

Heidi laughed.

"I'm all set on therapy. I used Eric's AmEx to furnish the new house."

I bit my lip.

"Seriously," she said, moving a bite of egg around on her plate. "I'm better off without that dodo anyway. He'll learn. The new model will only be fun for so long, then he'll come crawling back to me."

"Would you want to get back together with him?" I asked, more than a little surprised.

Heidi set her fork down. Her hands went to work smoothing the table cloth on either side of her plate.

"When I said, 'Til death do us part,' I meant it," she said earnestly. "And since murder is a sin, I'll just have to wait until he comes to his senses."

She looked around as if searching for our waitress, and I worried that she'd order another drink. I waved the busboy over to refill our coffee cups and water glasses.

"Well," I said, trying to decide how to steer the conversation onto a less fraught subject, "I'm glad you have the job at the animal rescue. You'll be so much better in that position than I was."

"I'm sure you were fine," Heidi said magnanimously. "But I can't wait to get started making changes."

I bit my lip again.

"Just remember, Heidi," I cautioned her. "You're dealing with old school Connecticut folk here. Change is a thing best approached slowly. Really, I found…"

Heidi reached over and patted my hand.

"Don't you worry! Don't you remember a *thing* from our college days? I am the absolute *soul* of diplomacy!"

I swirled the last of my eggs in Hollandaise sauce and shoveled them into my mouth before I could comment.

Luckily, Heidi wanted to walk and window shop, so I didn't have to worry about her getting behind the wheel of her Volvo too soon after drinking her brunch. An edge of worry had crept into my mind, though: what if the board of the animal rescue league had just hired a raging alcoholic on my recommendation? In the face of her divorce, Heidi appeared to be marinating in both denial and booze. I couldn't fault her, really—at least it seemed she'd yet to go fuck a stranger on the beach or dispose of expensive jewelry in the surf—but still. Maybe it hadn't been such a great idea to bring her so impulsively into my place of employment. It was the first real job I'd had in nearly twenty years. I didn't want to screw it up.

At a boutique I deliberately avoided since coming to terms with my new financial reality, I watched Heidi purchase a pile of summer clothes in various shades of pink. I couldn't help but think how obvious an act of rebellion her daughter's sense of style was. As Heidi handed over a credit card, I winked at her.

"Eric's AmEx?"

She shook her head.

"Oh no, sweetheart—he shut that down after the furniture incident. But I'm a modern woman! I have a job now!"

I wondered if she'd been listening when the board discussed salary, but for the umpteenth time that morning, I held my tongue. There was so much in that last statement of hers that made me sad. Sad, and angry. When we'd been students at Mount Holyoke, we'd considered ourselves modern women. Feminists. Independent. Hell, we wore combat boots with our miniskirts. We listened to Michelle Shocked.

We'd had it all mapped out, these lives we would create that would be so different from the lives our mothers and grandmothers had had no choice but to accept. How had we gone so far wrong that charging a pile of pink attire to one's own credit card at midlife could ever be considered a point of pride? And why did I find Heidi's state of being so pathetic, when I myself had been in her shoes not too long ago? Was it just human nature to only see in others the flaws that flourished within ourselves?

While Heidi's purchases were carefully wrapped and bagged, I stepped outside to check my phone. Part of me, I think, was hoping to hear from Max, and how ridiculous a wish was that? He'd rarely texted me under the best of circumstances, and then only when he wanted new lacrosse gear or some other expensive items. Indeed, a scroll through my phone told me it had been ages since he'd texted, and then only when he'd seen a new helmet he *had to* have.

There was a message from Nate featuring a photo of his living room stacked high with boxes ready for the move and the caption: *Shit just got real.*

I smiled and sent assorted emoji in reply.

A text from Finn confirmed he'd planned another paragliding escape…in Oklahoma.

Oklahoma????? I replied.

Lastly, a pic from Tamara showed a certified letter she'd signed for on my behalf. I tried to guess what it might be regarding, but came up empty and more than a little bit worried. I was all set on surprises of late.

I helped Heidi carry her bags back to her car, then checked the time. Two and a half hours until I needed to pick Eli up from school. I was tempted to swing by Finn's place, but knew the responsible thing would be to head back to Tamara's, take Sammie for a walk, and find out what the certified letter was all about.

"Toodle-oo, colleague!" Heidi called, waving her fingers out the window as she pulled away from the curb. "See you at work!"

What—*oh, what*—had I gotten myself into?

Chapter **Five**

The certified letter was an interesting one.

It came from the offices of Fisher & Webb, the Wolcott family attorneys. Kitty had specified that I not attend her funeral, but that Eli and Max be allowed to attend in the company of their uncles. My presence, however, was requested at the house for the reading of the will. Immediately, I felt a sense of dread. Would Kitty have directed her executors to stop funding the boys' education? Probably not. But I had no doubt there would be some form of game-playing or manipulation in this exercise. Perhaps she figured death would leave her free to tie as many strings as she liked to whatever bequests she left the living.

Whatever the particulars, I knew one thing: this would not go well.

"Un-fucking-believable," Tamara said. She and the boys had joined me and Sammie for our walk on the trails behind the house. "Even from the grave, that bitch plays cat and mouse."

"Are we really surprised?"

We both laughed.

"Okay, no," Tam conceded. "And what's the deal with Finn?"

"I guess he didn't get enough of paragliding in South America. He's off to some place in Oklahoma for something called a fly-in."

"Oklahoma? Who the hell goes to Oklahoma for vacation?"

"Well apparently," I laughed, "rich, prematurely-retired paragliding enthusiasts do."

"Trouble in paradise?" Tamara asked, pausing on the path.

"What? No!" I made a face at her, then pushed ahead. I could hear the boys and Sammie further up, but I'd lost sight of them. "I have to work, but he can do whatever he likes. It's not like we're joined at the hip or something."

"He certainly *does* do whatever he likes, doesn't he?

Have you two talked about the future at all?"

"The future?" I sputtered. "C'mon, Tam. Think about how the past year has gone. I'm still just trying to put one foot in front of the other here."

"Yeah, but let's be honest. No matter how great the sex is, there comes a point where you have to wonder where things are leading. Right?"

Warhol bounded back down the path, holding something out in front of him as he ran. I silently thanked him. *Saved by the bell.*

"Mom, LOOK!" he cried.

"Aw, fuck," Tamara replied.

I realized he was holding was the largest bullfrog I'd ever seen. Seriously. It had to be almost as big as the kid in whose muddy paws it was clutched. And it looked almost as startled as I felt.

"What have we talked about?" Tamara prompted her son.

"Animals are friends and we have to be gentle," he parroted dejectedly.

"Right. Now give it here."

Tamara took the frog from Warhol while I—a woman who had just signed on for a job that involved wading through animal feces on the daily—wrinkled my nose instinctively. I watched as she left the path and lowered the creature gently into the tall grass alongside the pond.

"Damn, you're a better woman than I."

She grinned at me as she wiped her hands on her jeans.

"If the little bastard comes back with a snake, all bets are off." As we resumed our walk, she continued, "So, I know you thought you were saved by the frog, but seriously—what's the plan with you and Finn?"

"I don't think there is a plan," I said. "Not just yet, anyway. I enjoy his company..."

"Enjoy his company!" Tamara mimicked, sticking her nose haughtily in the air.

I laughed.

"Okay, *I soak my panties at the mere thought of him.* Is that better?"

"More accurate," she grinned. "Go on..."

"Well, Finn is amazing. But a future together? I don't even know how to begin thinking about that. I'm still reeling from eighteen years with a man who fucked himself to death in bed with our kids' nanny. I'm pharmaceutical-free for the first time in ages. I'm so broke it hurts. And I love Finn—really, I do—but sometimes it just pisses me off, the way he's so free. And I know that's not fair. We both made our choices. He earned the life he's got. But at the same time, it's hard. It's not like when you're young and just starting out with someone and you have this sense that whatever you build, you build it together. There's an imbalance in this relationship that I'm almost afraid to acknowledge. I feel like my life is nothing but baggage and responsibility, while Finn's life is all paragliding and surfing and just taking off whenever he pleases."

"I get that," Tamara said. "I am kind of glad Howard and I got together when we did, back when we were both young and stupid and scraping by month-to-month. I'm not sure I'd feel as okay about staying home with the kids if not for the fact that I know Howard's career wouldn't have taken off without my support. It's been teamwork all the way.

"But you know, Finn's life is changing. Didn't he mention Molly might come out here for college? That's huge. Frankly, I'm not surprised he's taking off on another paragliding trip. I mean, it's gotta be a fucking trip for him to even wrap his head around the idea that his style might be cramped by having a teenage girl in his life, you know?"

I laughed. I had been thinking the very same thing.

"Anyway," she went on. "He knows what a massive fucking boatload of baggage you come with. You've given the dude plenty of opportunities to bolt. And for whatever reason, he still wants to be with you. I think at some point, you just have to accept that he's your lobster."

The *Friends* reference made me laugh again. I loved that my history with this woman went back so far, we had our own language, silly inside jokes that could instantly conjure up a Lisa Kudrow character and the notion of crustaceans bonding for life.

"He's my lobster," I agreed. "But what if I'm more seagull than lobster. Or maybe he'd be the seagull, and I'd be the lobster..."

"Okay, I think we're taking this metaphor way off track here."

"You know what I mean. We're fine when we're alone together, me and Finn. Sure. But what if our realities don't mesh? What's that saying? A bird may fall in love with a fish, but where would they live?"

Tamara sighed.

"I don't know. I guess I sort of had that feeling back in the beginning, when everything was going great with Howard, and then I learned he was bisexual. It really fucked with my head, you know? I mean, I didn't have any problem with it theoretically, but I worried that maybe in practice, it would be an issue down the road. Like, he'd get tired of always having clam on the menu, and start craving sausage?"

I doubled over in hysterics.

"Tam, you have such a way with words. You're a goddamned poet."

"Thank you." She punched my arm. "You know what I mean, though. That would have been a deal breaker for some people. But I just figured the way Howard and I loved each other was a rare enough thing that we'd work it out, and it would be worth it. And you know what? It has been. Every fucking crazy minute of my life with that man has been an adventure I wouldn't trade for anything in the world. I mean, sure—he steals my mascara, and every now and then there's gay porn on my iPad. But whose marriage is perfect?"

I shook my head.

"I think maybe that's the thing that worries me. My marriage was the opposite of perfect, but man, did we put on a show. I disappeared. I was consumed by Skip and his world. And still, I stayed. I wonder sometimes what would have happened if he'd lived. Would I have had the nerve to go through with the divorce?"

We emerged from the path, and Tamara turned to face me.

"The 'what ifs' will kill you. You've gotta let go of that shit. Okay? It'll kill you, and it doesn't even matter. You're right here, right now. Day One, baby. Let Finn go on his little paragliding adventure. You go shovel dogshit and kitty litter. When he comes back, you can fuck each other's brains out and go from there."

"You always come up with the best plans," I told Tamara honestly.

"It's a fucking gift, I tell you," she winked.

She turned her attention to the boys in the open meadow before us. They were playing a wild game of tag with Sammie, and the Spring thaw had left them all covered in mud.

"Look at those little fuckers," she said affectionately. "Have you ever seen anything more disgustingly adorable?"

I shook my head and smiled.

"Honestly? I have not. But I'm still damn glad the fur kid is the only one I'll have to bathe."

****

I stayed at Finn's house the night before he left for Oklahoma. The sounds of the ocean came gently through the sliding glass doors, which stood slightly open. The breeze off the water was chilly, but Finn had kept the fireplace going overnight. Between that and the heat his lovely body gave off like a furnace, I'd stayed warm. It was like camping, only with all the comforts of a multi-million-dollar oceanfront estate.

I woke before dawn to a nibbling at the base of my neck. Finn curled more tightly around me, spooning me as I nestled beneath the comforter. We made love in that slow, lazy way I'd come to think of as a weekend morning privilege, a delight like pancakes with maple syrup…but sweeter. Afterward, I dozed off again, wrapped in Finn's arms. His orange tomcat, Oscar Wilde, hopped up and curled contentedly under my chin. On the floor beside the bed, Sammie yawned and stretched and went back to sleep as well.

When at last I woke fully, the sky outside was light, but rain was falling. I slid my hand over to Finn's side of the bed and found the sheets cool and empty.

"Rise and shine, sleepyhead," he said from the doorway.

I realized he was dressed and ready for his trip. I sat up and he kissed me. I missed him already.

He led me to the master bath, where I saw he'd filled the Jacuzzi tub. A cup of coffee waited for me, and there, too, the gas fireplace was lit and the sound of the surf came through the open doors.

"The best of all worlds," he said, taking my robe from me and hanging it up. I stepped into the hot water and sank down, keeping my eyes on his.

"Are you trying to distract me from your departure?" I asked.

"I am," he replied. "Is it working?"

I leaned forward and took a sip of coffee, then sank back

into the tub. The bubbling water rose to my chin.

"Pretty much," I acknowledged.

He crouched down and kissed me.

"I'll be back in a week. Carla's coming at noon, so you might want to be dressed by then. She'll do the dishes and laundry, so leave that stuff, okay?"

"Okay," I smiled, resisting the urge to ask if I could bring Carla home with me when I left.

"You sure you don't want to come?"

"It's not that I don't want to…"

"Yeah, yeah. Work. I kinda remember how that goes." He winked. "I love you, Eve."

I rose up on my knees and leaned in to kiss him again.

"I love you, Finn."

He stood, and I laughed as I sank back down into the bath.

"What…?" he began, then he caught a glimpse of himself in the mirror. My breasts had left two distinct wet spots on his shirt.

"I guess I'd better go change," he said, grinning widely. "And then I'm outta here. For real. Before this mermaid I know drags me into her lair."

****

Any time I spent at Finn's house was like going on a mini-vacation, I realized. His home had all the appointments of a fine resort—spectacular view, private beach, pristine accommodations—and I never had to lift a finger. Finn's housekeeper, Carla, took care of all the details, and the house itself was like something out of a 007 movie. When I entered a room, lights came on and the temperature adjusted to preferences I'd set earlier. I never had to worry about forgetting to turn the lights off, either, because the house took care of that, too. A simple voice command, and the music of my choice sounded through the speakers in whatever room I occupied. Wine and food were always just the perfect temperature. It was delightful, but also somehow unsettling.

The contrast when I would return to Tamara's house—where children always ran riot, Howard might be singing (badly) while he cooked, and Tam was forever letting F-bombs fly—was always stark, but I began to realize I preferred the wild unpredictability of Tamara and Howard's place to the sterile certainty of Finn's. Even Nana's cottage, where faucets dripped and floors slanted and I was always either too hot or too cold, felt more like home to me than I imagined Finn's ever would. On the drive back from Westerly, I thought of my conversation with Tamara, how she'd seemed surprised that Finn and I hadn't discussed a future together, not in any concrete terms. I realized part of it was that, while Finn's world was a very nice place to visit, I wasn't sure I could live there. And if he liked everything so perfectly neat and tidy, how would he ever fit into my messy life?

I drove past Tamara and Howard's driveway, continuing on to the house that now officially belonged to Nate and Ian. They wouldn't arrive until the next day, but the attorney who'd handled the closing was a friend of the family, and he'd turned the keys over to Tamara so the cleaning could begin. When I stepped through the door, I realized how fully anyone involved with this house would have their work cut out for them.

It was pretty much as Tam and Howard had described it, yet some things need to be seen to be believed. Just as it appeared from outside, the house had great lines inside. The split-level floor plan and wide-beamed ceilings had potential. The rest, though?

I couldn't quite imagine how Nate had sold Ian on the place. Nate had vision Ian lacked, and if ever a house required vision, it was this one.

The focal point of the main floor was a massive fireplace running the length of the living room and wrapping around to the dining room, constructed entirely of what appeared to be lava rocks. What might have looked interesting for five minutes in 1969 had become over the years a giant magnet for dust and cobwebs that could never, by any human means, be fully removed. I imagined some of the grey fuzz coating the thing was older than any of us standing there in the house.

The kitchen, however, had suffered a redo sometime in the '80's. It was a hybrid of Miami Vice and Golden Girls, all pink and teal geometric wallpaper with a bit of gold foil thrown in here and there. The backsplash was mirrored.

"Horrific, right?" Howard said, following my eyes. "How the hell are you supposed to do lines from a vertical surface?"

Tamara emerged from a bathroom wearing rubber gloves and carrying a bucket of filthy water.

"Look at me," she said. "I brought cleaning supplies to a blowtorch party."

"Where should I start?" I asked. "Want me to try sucking some of the dust off the lava wall with a vacuum cleaner?"

Tamara sighed.

"I just did that."

"Oh. Well. I'm sure it's much better than it was."

I took the bucket from Tamara and refilled it with clean soapy water in the kitchen sink, then followed her upstairs. I went to work on one bathroom while she tackled the other. The rooms were back-to-back, so when Tamara took an incoming phone call, I could hear almost everything. I set my sponge down and took off my gloves. I went and stood in the doorway and waited for her to finish the call. When she stepped out into the hallway, her face was as white as mine felt.

"That was the doctor's office," she said.

"I know. I wasn't trying to listen, but..."

"They want me to come in, but I told them to tell me over the phone."

I nodded. I already knew.

"It's not good, is it?"

She shook her head.

"Not good," she agreed. "I'm almost two months pregnant..." she paused, shaking, "...and it seems I may have breast cancer."

Chapter **Six**

There are moments in life you always think will happen to someone else.

Someone else has their house burned down.

Someone else loses their spouse to a drunk driver.

Someone else is diagnosed with cancer.

We all think we are immune to disaster. It's how we make life bearable, I suppose. How we manage to drag our asses out of bed every morning and put one foot in front of the other. How we weather the ups and downs. A spouse cheats and we're devastated, but then we hear about this person whose child just died, or that person who just learned he has M.S. We measure our tragedies in degrees, and as long as someone else has it worse, we decide we're okay, we can make it through.

And in fairness, even now, I was not the one hearing the C-word over the phone. It was not my breasts harboring the enemy. Nor—holy shit—was it my womb cradling yet another new life in the midst of a health crisis.

But Tamara.

My best friend.

For the first time in my life, I wished the greater tragedy were mine. I wished I could do something more than just open my arms and fold her in.

"Don't you fucking dare make me cry," she said.

"Who, me? No way. Let's just... What, exactly, did they say?"

"That I'm fucked, and I'm fucked," Tamara snorted.

"Yeah, but... Stage? Prognosis? Treatment?"

She shook free of me, clearly annoyed.

"I don't fucking know. The doctor was on the phone for a whopping ninety seconds. Probably has a tee time to get to."

"But..."

"I have an appointment. Monday."

"Monday," I echoed.

"Yeah," Tamara said, sitting down at the top of the staircase. "Like, first fucking available appointment. I guess they give those to the dead women walking."

"Oh Tam, don't…"

I put my hand on her shoulder, and she shrugged it off. Downstairs, the front door opened, and the sound of small boys yelling echoed throughout the empty house. I heard Howard yelling back at the boys, threatening them with time out if they tracked mud inside. Then I heard him gasp.

"Ladies! You have to come down here," he called up the stairs. "I think Ian's parents have arrived with the, um, motor home."

Tamara gave me a withering stare as she rose.

"Not a word to anyone," she said.

"You have to tell Howard," I countered automatically.

"I will," she promised. "But not now."

I watched her make her way down the stairs, somewhat surprised at how steady she looked when I felt brutally weak in the knees. I followed several paces behind, and when we reached the front steps, we nearly crashed into Howard.

There we all stood, mouths agape.

The motor home—what else was one to call it?— occupied the entire driveway. And I mean 'occupied' in an invading-foreign-troops sort of way.

It took up the whole damn space, and it looked utterly alien and imposing. The thing was the size of an eighteen-wheeler, a gleaming stainless steel-sided behemoth emblazoned with the image of a wildly waving American flag and a vengeful-looking eagle. The rig was so large, the silver Hummer towed behind it (also emblazoned with the same flag and eagle) looked small. I heard the hiss of air compression as a door opened, and I realized all else was strangely silent. Tamara and Howard's brood of wild boys stood in a line, perfectly still, staring. It was as if a space ship had landed and we were all waiting to see what strange extra-terrestrial creatures would emerge.

The cowboy boot that touched down seemed an extension of the vehicle, shiny and gaudy. And then there he was: The Chicken King. Tall, wide, red-faced. I recognized him immediately from the commercials. I almost expected him to open his mouth and offer, *"More cluck-cluck-cluck for your buck-buck-buck!"* He turned back toward the motor home and held out his hand, and a smaller hand reached out and settled in his palm. Very long, very bright red fingernails were followed by a blinding array of rings, and then a petite figure (presumably The Chicken Queen) came into view.

She had fiery red hair piled high on her head, and what had to be the largest fake breasts I had ever seen. As she stepped forward, I realized she had the rear end to balance them out, yet her waist was alarmingly small. She called to mind images I'd seen of women who'd corset-trained to the point of rearranging internal organs and putting their spines in danger of snapping. It was as though a short, sixty-something incarnation of Jessica Rabbit had appeared before us.

I blinked and cast a sideways glance at Tamara, and found her jaw had literally dropped. I elbowed her and she closed her mouth.

"Y'all must be Nate's family?" The Chicken King said, stepping forward and extending a meaty hand. "I'm Wolf, and this is Kandie."

"That's Kandie with a 'K' at the start, and an 'I—E' at the finish," she clarified, stepping forward and winking.

"Why doesn't she just spell out the whole damn thing," Tamara mumbled quietly, and I elbowed her again.

For a painfully awkward moment, Howard and Wolf faced off, sizing each other up.

"You must be one of Nate's, ah, *friends*?" Wolf guessed at last.

Tamara pushed forward and shook Wolf's hand vigorously.

"Actually, this is my husband, Howard. I'm Tamara, Nate's sister. And this is Eve."

I shook Wolf's outstretched hand, then was startled to find myself pulled into Kandie's embrace. Her perfume overwhelmed me as she planted damp kisses on each of my cheeks. She subjected Tamara to the same treatment. Tam and Howard's boys, perhaps fearing they'd be next, broke their silent ranks and scattered. Normalcy returned as they found sticks and began whacking each other in the sort of war game their parents forbade. Howard's halfhearted calls for them to stop fell on deaf ears. Tamara invited Wolf and Kandie inside, and Howard and I trailed after them.

"Oh. Dear. Lord."

Kandie froze in the foyer, clapping a hand to her massive bosom.

"Yeah. It needs some work," Tamara acknowledged.

"Some work?" Kandie breathed. "*Some work?* It needs a natural disaster, God forgive me. Our Ian *bought* this?" She pawed at her husband's arm. "Oh, Wolfie—you have *got* to sit that boy down for a talking-to. He's clearly gone out of his mind, bless his poor little heart!"

"I'm sure Nate and Ian will transform the place," Tamara said, bristling. "They've got vision."

"Vision? *Vision?*" Kandie cried. "What they need is a *bulldozer!*"

"Now, Pet," Wolf said, settling his large hand on his wife's larger derriere, "just hold your horses. Ain't nothin' been done that can't be fixed."

"Can't be fixed? *Can't be fixed?*" Kandie retorted, her

voice increasing in pitch.

She was clearly only getting more stirred up, while I was starting to get the idea that we'd have to endure every word she felt inclined to speak not once, but twice.

Bless our own poor little hearts.

"Oh, Wolfie, just look at this place!" she lamented, draping a hand heavily over her husband's arm, as if she required physical support. "*Just look!* Honestly, ever since Ian left Florida, it just keeps getting worse…"

I could practically see steam coming out of Tamara's ears, and I realized she was getting the same subtext I inferred. In Florida, Nate had told us, Ian had been engaged to a woman and poised to take over the family business. Instead, he came out as gay, moved to the San Francisco, established his own career, and built a life with Nate. None of which, it seemed, fit with Wolf and Kandie's plans for their only child.

"How about a drink?" Howard, in his infinite wisdom, suggested.

"Oh, merciful Jesus, yes!" Kandie agreed, moving her hand from Wolf's arm to Howard's. The relief that briefly flooded her face disappeared as she looked around again, perhaps contemplating the horror of cocktail hour in her present surroundings. "But why don't y'all come into the motor home? We've got a bar there. And it's…*tidy*."

So it was that we found ourselves boarding the behemoth. Tamara paused long enough to threaten her children with death if they either left the yard or brought their mucky little selves into the motor home, then climbed the steps after me.

It was like nothing I'd ever seen before.

It was huge and modern and brightly lit by recessed lighting overhead and in every imaginable nook and cranny. There was granite and leather and stainless steel and plush carpeting everywhere. A plastic vase of fake flowers on the table and another on a countertop gave the space a tacky showroom look.

"All the comforts of home," Kandie announced proudly. She was noticeably more relaxed in this space. "Go on and take a load off. Make yourselves at home."

She settled into a plush reclining chair and drummed her long nails loudly on the table beside her. Wolf pressed a button and a fully-stocked bar rose from beneath a stretch of granite. He mixed and garnished a pink beverage of some sort so quickly, delivering it swiftly to Kandie, the act seemed subconscious. As Kandie took a long first sip, he took drink orders from the rest of us.

"Nothing for me, thanks," Tamara said. "Too much to do today."

Her hand, though, went instinctively to her belly, and I could see the gears turning in her mind: how many drinks had she consumed these past couple months, before she knew there was a tiny life taking hold within her?

"I'll pass too," I said. "I need to take Eli shopping later."

Kandie let out a hoot.

"Well, they told me y'all were a bunch of stiffs up here in New England! I have to say, though, I don't know how you can look at a house like that and not just get down on your knees and thank the good Lord for John Barleycorn." She took another slurp of her drink. "Wolfie, baby, thanks for this—otherwise it might be *weeks* before I could sleep again, knowing our boy actually bought that godawful place. *Weeks!*"

"Where are you from, originally?" Tamara asked, sipping the glass of sparkling water Wolf handed her. "I can't quite place your accent."

"Oh, here and there," Kandie said, waving a hand in a dismissive spiral. "Been in good ol' Florida since I met Wolfie back in 1972, so I like to think of myself as a regular ol' Cracker Girl."

"Cracker," Howard mused aloud, wrinkling his nose. "Isn't that a term that had something to do with slavery? Like, the way slaveholders would crack the whip in the fields?"

Kandie winked as if she and Howard were co-

conspirators.

"Where the government's true," she smiled, dipping a fingernail into her drink and spearing a cherry. She set her glass down on her cleavage as if it were a shelf.

"You know, you're going to have to excuse me," Tamara said. "I must've spent a bit too long with those cleaning products this morning. I'm feeling a bit nauseous."

"Me too," I said, standing alongside her. Howard inhaled his drink and stood ready to follow us.

"Well, we're here to help," Wolf offered, setting his drink down and standing. In his cowboy boots, he towered over all of us. "We'll just settle in here—don't you worry about us. Go about your business, and let us know how we can pitch in."

"We won't be a bit of trouble," Kandie added. She remained seated, as if holding court. Her drink jiggled on her chest. "Lord knows, our Ian doesn't need any more *strife!*"

I practically pushed Tamara out the door before she could speak, and I dragged Howard after me. Even halfway up the path to the house, we could hear the door of the motor home hiss shut.

"Lord knows, our Ian doesn't need any more strife!" Tamara mimicked as we walked inside. "I imagine 'strife' is their nickname for my brother? Fucking rednecks. Or whatever the hell they are. I mean, really—what *are* they? Aside from a

cautionary tale about what happens when trash makes money?"

Howard massaged her shoulders.

"You really should have a drink, darling," he said.

Tamara and I exchanged a glance. I pulled my phone from my pocket and pretended to marvel at the time.

"I hate to clean toilets and meet white trash and run," I quipped, "but Sammie needs a walk, and Eli and I have a date to shop for running shoes. So I'm off!"

Howard looked bewildered as I kissed his cheek, then pulled Tamara in for a long hug.

"I love you," I whispered in her ear.

"Not a word to Nate," she whispered back. "Not yet, okay?"

"Okay," I agreed solemnly. "You'll talk to Howard?"

"Right now," she promised, squeezing my hand.

And then I headed out the door before the tears I felt rising within me could escape.

****

Shopping for running shoes with Eli was a good distraction, if only temporarily. Freya came along with us, and I tried to get used to the familiar way she and Eli had with each other. It was wonderful to see him happy, and I loved the way Freya seemed to appreciate his quirks just as I'd always hoped someone would. Still, it took some getting used to, the idea that this tall, lanky creature on the brink of manhood was my son, and the heavily made-up young woman in ripped tights and Doc Martens was his girlfriend. It stood to reason that this all meant I was getting O-L-D, yet while they walked ahead of me at the outlet mall, I exchanged flirty texts with Finn, who'd arrived in Oklahoma.

I was doing the midlife crisis up admirably.

I didn't mention Tamara's news to Finn, partly because I wasn't sure if her request for my silence was just for Nate's sake or if it extended to others, and partly because text seemed a lousy medium for such a conversation. I did feel a little twinge as we texted back and forth, the light banter incongruous with what I knew and felt. What poor timing for Finn to leave! I'd have given anything to have known that I'd be spending the evening curled up with him and a bottle of wine, able to share this burden.

Instead, it was Sammie and a novel I curled up with later. I read the same paragraph over and over again, then gave up. I hadn't heard from Tamara, and I didn't want to pester her with texts, but the truth was, I couldn't stop thinking of her. I longed to have a real conversation about things, to find out what she was thinking.

The reality that she was both pregnant and had breast cancer had sunk in, and I wondered at the implications. Could she keep the pregnancy and still have cancer treatment? Was it a choice between the baby's health and her own? And how did she feel about this pregnancy independent of the cancer? She and Howard loved children, sure, but they already had a large family, and she hadn't mentioned anything to me about expanding their brood further. Was this in the cards?

I made myself a cup of camomile tea and took it outside, wrapping up in a wool blanket as I went. The sky was stark black, and the stars shone brightly. At the pond behind the cottage, frogs chirped and croaked loudly. Somewhere overhead, a pair of owls called back and forth to one another. I kept Sammie on leash, lest he go off after one of the skunks that nested under the shed. He settled at my feet with a sigh, as if he suspected he were being deprived of a good time. I leaned forward in my Adirondack chair and scratched his ears, hoping that at least somewhat made up for it. I texted Max, expecting no reply. Finn texted, looking to talk, but I told him I was tired and ready for sleep, which was partially true.

Tired was exactly how I felt.

Tired of so much change. Tired of all the unexpected curve balls. Tired of feeling so much of life was painfully beyond my control.

I thought of Tamara and realized I was going to have to get my shit together. If I felt tired, how must she feel? Four kids under age eight, a never-ending swirl of family activity, and now cancer coupled with a pregnancy. She was going to need support, which meant I was going to have to grow a fucking spine.

I took a long sip of my tea, which was rapidly cooling in the evening air.

"That's it, you know, Sammie?" I mused aloud, and my canine companion tipped his head at me. "I've had a pity party for a while now, all woe-is-me and hanging on by a thin thread. It's gotta end. Skip's dead and gone. Now Kitty is too. If that doesn't prove we're all mortal, I don't know what does. And now Tamara…"

The tears overwhelmed me in a sudden wave. Everything I couldn't bear to think hit me at once. I doubled over, sobbing.

Sammie leapt up and licked at my tears. My breath caught in my throat, and I laughed for a moment, then cried harder. I clutched at the dog, his body wagging in my arms as if propelled by his tail. I wondered briefly if this had been Finn's plan, to provide me with a companion so he'd be free to take off at will. I dismissed the idea as quickly as it had arrived. Finn had wanted me to go with him, hadn't he? It wasn't his fault that I was anchored here by responsibilities.

And yet, as my tears subsided and I led Sammie back into the cottage, I couldn't help but recognize the familiar feeling, that one I'd lived with so long in my marriage to Skip. It was the sense of being partnered, yet alone—almost as if the relationship I was in were a technicality, or a thing intended for the convenience and comfort of my partner, but not for me.

Again, I brushed the idea away. Surely this was just what came of being married to someone like Skip for so long. Old feelings and fears were lingering. If I wasn't careful, I could worry them into far more than they were.

I paused before the wood stove, deciding the evening was warm enough that I would let the fire burn out. As I padded into the bedroom, my phone buzzed with an incoming text.

From Finn.

Goodnight, Eve. I love you and miss you.

I smiled, feeling my worries vanish.

Damn, I was easily appeased.

Goodnight, Finn. I texted back. *I love you and miss you too.*

****

The next morning, Tam summoned me to the main house to greet Nate and Ian.

She texted: *The fucking chicken-chokers have Ian all bent about the new place. I'm insisting on neutral turf for their arrival.*

I headed up the hill, throwing a frisbee for Sammie so he'd tire himself out along the way. It was wishful thinking. His size—100 lbs. and growing—made me forget sometimes that he was still a puppy, blessed with boundless energy. Luckily, though, his size also meant he could withstand the exuberant affections of Tam's boys. They launched themselves off the porch as we approached, yelling, "Sammie!" The dog wagged his tail madly and charged toward his little buddies.

Inside, Tamara shared the kitchen with Meri, the personal chef who came every so often to stock the freezer and help feed the family when it was a full house. The kitchen smelled of cinnamon and nutmeg.

"Hello, Eve!" Meri called, pouring a cup of coffee and handing it to me.

"Hello, Meri! And thank you. It smells like heaven in here. What on earth are you making?"

"Everything!" Tamara grinned, kissing me on the cheek. "My brother is moving in next door, and not even the Chicken

King and Queen can ruin it for me."

"Cinnamon buns are in the oven," Meri said. "Nate's favorite. And I'm working on that vegan sausage Ian likes."

"I thought Ian preferred Nate's vegan sausage?" Howard smirked, gliding into the room.

"Oh man," Tamara sighed, kissing her husband on the cheek. "It's a good thing you gave me, like, a gazillion orgasms last night."

She handed me a stack of dishes and we headed into the dining room.

"You seem awfully chipper this morning," I said suspiciously.

"You mean, for a dead woman walking?"

"Stop!"

"I wasn't kidding about those orgasms," she said slyly. "Howard wanted to 'talk' last night, so I just sat on his face instead. I tell you, that is the best way for a married mother of four to get a quiet moment."

I laughed in spite of myself, but as I followed her around the table, setting plates down on the placemats one pace behind her, I wondered what Tam was really feeling.

"Are you doing that thing where you act all flippant so no one will know you want to cry?"

She shook her head.

"Nope. I'm doing that thing where I pretend I'm a zen fucking Buddhist and stay totally in the present moment," she said, circling the table once more with silverware. "No sense doing otherwise, right? I'll get information on Monday, and I'll deal with it then. In the meantime, Nate and Ian are moving in *right next door*, and I get to meet the little hellions they've adopted, and I'll have the vast majority of people I love all right here in my little corner of the world. So really, I'd have to be an asshole not to appreciate that."

I set down the last of the dishes I was holding and gave her a quick hug.

"This is why I love you," I said. "Well, one of the three million reasons."

"The invasion's begun," Howard said, popping his head into the dining room. "A Hummer just drove over our Prius, and I think I see Ian's Audi behind it."

We stepped out onto the porch, and sure enough, there they were.

Kandie was decked out in the sort of frilly floral ensemble that reminded me of the dresses I'd been forced to wear on Easter as a child, only her plunging neckline exposed far more cleavage than I could ever imagine having, never mind putting on display. Wolf wore the deep cobalt blue jeans, button-down denim shirt and cowboy boots that I was beginning to understand were his uniform. Behind them, Nate and Ian emerged from their car, both in khakis and Oxford shirts, though Nate's shirt had a multicolored stripe to it, while Ian's was classic blue.

And then the twins stepped from the car.

They were twelve going on twenty-five, each in a micro-mini skirt and lace top fitted enough to reveal their tiny, neon-colored bras beneath. Long earrings dangled against their cheeks, and they flipped their hair from side to side like nervous horses twitching their tails. They wore dark lipstick and eyeliner, and one of them snapped her bubble gum so loudly, I could hear it clear across the lawn.

Kandie tottered over to Ian, the heels of her shoes sticking in the damp earth. She kissed his cheeks and then hung on his arm, pulling him away from Nate. I caught the sidelong glances that both Wolf and Nate cast their way. The group headed to the house, the twins dragging behind as if marching to their own execution.

After a round of greetings and hugs, Nate reached out to the twins and ushered them forward.

"Everyone, meet Amber and Brandi," he said. "Ladies, this is...*everyone*."

As the rest of the group took turns introducing themselves, Howard leaned in and whispered in my ear.

"It's not like adopting cats, is it?" he mused. "If they come with stripper names, you can't change them, eh?"

I elbowed him and tried not to laugh. I caught sight of Eli in the doorway and reminded myself that these girls, no matter how tough they looked, were younger than he was, and there was no guessing what they'd been through in their young lives.

"I'm Eve," I said, extending a hand they pointedly ignored. "And that's my son, Eli. He goes to Pinecroft, where you'll be starting school."

"Oh, joy," Brandi hissed under her breath. Her twin giggled. I bit my tongue.

We all made our way into the dining room and sat down for brunch. Kandie clucked appreciatively over the food, until she realized most of it was vegan. She recoiled as if bitten by a dish of vegan sausage, passing it quickly to Wolf. He poked at the contents of the serving dish, then sent it on its way.

"Never could understand that," he commented. "Why be a vegetarian and then try to make all your food taste like meat? Damn foolish. Anyway, if God wanted us to eat only plants, he wouldn't have given us these canine choppers." He flashed a toothy grin, then patted his large belly. "There's meat at every meal at our house. If our boy hadn't passed on it all the time, he might've grown up big and strong like his old man."

Silence fell and Ian's face flushed bright red. Nate looked ready to fight. The twins broke the silence, snickering.

"Wolfie," Kandie cooed, putting a hand to her husband's shoulder. "Our Ian has just had a long, stressful trip, and now he's got that hideous house to deal with. I mean, *truly*—I didn't sleep a wink last night thinking about that mess! *Not a wink!* Let's not add to his burden, dear. He's a grown man now. He can eat whatever he likes." She lowered her voice, then added, "Though I'm not sure why he wouldn't like a lovely piece of meat now and then…"

I felt it coming even before Nate opened his mouth.

"Oh, he likes a lovely piece of meat now and then," he muttered under his breath.

The twins erupted in laughter. Eli's jaw dropped. Tamara and Howard hooted.

"I'm sorry, I didn't catch that?" Kandie commented, looking confused.

Wolf, however, had clearly caught it. His face turned several shades redder than its usual hue. He shot his son a withering glance, and Ian dropped his head.

"Buns?" Meri offered, appearing in the doorway with a tray.

The laughter resumed. Wolf and Kandie grew silent, draining their mimosas.

I cleared my throat and tried to change the subject.

"So," I began, addressing Ian's parents, "will you stay long enough to do some sightseeing, or are you heading back to Florida right away?"

Kandie blinked.

"Why on earth would we be heading back to Florida right away?"

"Um…I…ah…thought you were bringing the mobile home for Nate and Ian and the girls to use during the renovation?" I replied, a questioning note edging out what I'd thought was understood.

"Well yes, of course," Kandie said. "But there's enough room for everyone. We wouldn't just leave our boy to deal with that horrible house all by himself!"

I saw Nate's eyes widen and a glance pass between him and Tamara. Clearly he was not aware that this was the plan. He tipped his head at Ian, who again looked down.

"Well, he won't be renovating the house *all by himself*, will he?" Tamara asked, a hard edge to her voice. "He'll be doing it *with his husband*."

Wolf snorted and jabbed his fork at his plate, spearing a bite of asparagus and shoveling it into his mouth. The tension in the room grew, and excitement passed between the twins as clearly as an electrical current. Glances darted around the table like balls in a pinball machine.

"Everyone needs a hand now and then, and that's what family's for," Kandie said with finality. "We'll be staying to help our boy."

I looked over at Nate, and could read in his very posture all the concerns running through his mind. He looked ready to flee.

"Well then," Howard said, clearing his throat and raising his glass. "Here's to family, and to new beginnings!"

As the rest of us toasted, I saw Ian reach over and pat Nate's knee apologetically. He looked utterly crushed, and Nate didn't look much better.

I suspected this new beginning might be fraught with challenges.

Chapter **Seven**

Eli and I stretched following a quick run. Sammie ran in circles after his own tail, then darted off. I looked up and saw he'd gone to greet Tamara and Nate as they wandered down to the cottage.

"Let's have a proper hello, sis," Nate said, wrapping me in his arms.

"Oh! I'm so sweaty and gross!" I apologized.

Nate laughed and pinched his nose as he released me from the embrace.

"Sweetheart, I've always though girls stunk, but you *do* take the cake right now!" he grinned.

Eli high-fived Nate.

"How's it going at the house?" I asked, almost fearfully.

"How's it going?" Nate responded, settling into one Adirondack chair while Tam took the other. "If I can make it through this experience without committing either murder or suicide, I'll expect a medal."

"He did not know Ian's parents planned to stay," Tamara said, anticipating my question. "But apparently Ian did."

"Oh no," I said sympathetically. "I'm so sorry, Nate. Having met Ian's parents, though, I can see where he maybe was afraid to tell you."

"You think?" Nate quipped.

Tamara handed him a Thermos and he took a swig, then held it out to me.

"Vodka gimlet?" he offered.

I shook my head.

"No, and actually, hang on a minute. I've gotta run in for water. Tam, want anything?"

"No, thanks!"

I made a quick dash inside. Eli followed me. He filled his water bottle, then said, "I'm gonna head up to the house and take a shower. Can you give me a ride to Freya's in a bit?"

"Sure," I agreed.

I rejoined Tamara and Nate, and Eli waved goodbye and started up the hill.

"I brought Nate up to speed on my medical situation," Tam said once Eli was out of earshot.

Nate drew in a deep breath.

"I told her it was thoughtful of her to put my troubles into perspective, but I think she went a bit overboard."

"When have I ever done anything in a small way?" Tamara winked.

Their banter was no different than usual, but it fell flat today.

"I'm going to watch the kiddos while Tam's at her appointment on Monday," Nate explained. "At the very least, it will get me out of the Chicken Empire's takeover of my life for a bit."

"Can I go with you, Tam? I can cancel work."

"Thanks, sweetie, but no thanks. Howard's going to come with me. He's beside himself. Happy about the baby, but terrified about the cancer."

"In other words," Nate said, taking another swig from the Thermos, "he's a completely rational human being."

"So, you'll keep the pregnancy?" I said, knowing my words lacked tact, but that none was required with Tamara.

She nodded.

"Assuming it's possible, and the baby looks healthy. Really, I have no idea how this works. I caught Howard on

WebMD and told him to get the fuck off there before he terrifies himself. That shit's poison. Me? I'll wait for an actual doctor to give me specifics relative to my situation, you know?"

"Good call," I said.

We sat in silence for a moment, then I turned to Nate.

"The girls are…interesting," I said.

He laughed so hard, vodka nearly escaped his nose.

"That's one word for them," he said. "Honestly, they're hateful little bitches. I hope to hell the therapist we've lined up here can work magic, because I feel like I invited evil into our lives." He paused, looking contemplative. "Perhaps Ian brought his parents into the mix as payback."

"Have you never met them before?" I asked, incredulous. "You and Ian have been together nearly six years."

"They met us in Vegas once for Christmas—you know, the traditional Currier and Ives deal with dancers and gambling and cheap booze and buffets. In that context, they didn't seem all that over-the-top. But *dear Lord and bless my little heart*, it's a whole new world now, isn't it?"

"Ian's mother has assigned them to a little cubby on that bus that's identical to the one the twins will be occupying," Tamara said. "Right on down to the bunk beds. *Bunk beds!*"

"Bunk beds?" I exclaimed. "*Bunk beds?*"

"Well, now y'all sound just like her," Nate teased,

adopting an accent that approximated Kandie's, "what with all the repetition."

"Will you and Ian argue over who gets to be on top?" I teased back.

Nate sighed.

"Oh, Eve. I can't even joke about it. Let's focus on you, shall we? Where's the hottie? Tamara tried to tell me he's in *Oklahoma*, but that can't be right."

I laughed.

"Actually, that's right. Apparently there's some sort of paragliding thing in Oklahoma."

"And apparently, Eve and Finn have reached that point in their relationship where he starts doing that dickish guy thing and fleeing," Tamara chimed in.

Her comment caught me off guard.

Was that really what Finn was doing? Had I become a burden he needed to escape?

"Um, well, ah…" I explained. "I really think he just wanted to go to this fly-in thingy."

Nate and Tamara both nodded, their eyes averted from me in a way I wished I hadn't noticed.

My phone buzzed and I glanced down.

Finn had texted:

Great day of flying. Check out the pics. Gotta admit,

tho…I miss you!

"Speak of the devil," I said, somewhat defiantly.

I shared the accompanying photos with Nate and Tam, beautiful shots of multi-colored paragliders against blue sky.

"Aww, what a sweet flyboy you've got there," Nate commented.

He and Tamara stood.

"Gotta make a dinner plan," she said.

"And I've gotta get a shower," I said.

I kissed them quickly and watched them go on their way, but an uneasy feeling lingered. Nate was dealing with a major family crisis, Tamara a medical one.

Why had they both looked at *me* with pity as they left?

****

Monday was a doozy.

I arrived at work fifteen minutes early, and found Heidi was already there. My relief at her eagerness—and apparent sobriety—was short-lived.

"Happy Monday, colleague!" she sang. "I left a folder with some paperwork on your desk. If you could just fill out the volunteer evaluations and get them back to me by day's end, that would be great. It'll help me figure out the new schedule and placement." She sidled up to me and lowered her voice. "Oh, and you might want to tidy up your desk a bit. It was very difficult for me to find anything I needed."

I stared for a moment.

"What are you doing poking around my desk?" I asked at last.

Heidi looked perplexed.

"I needed to get working, and you weren't here. Don't worry. I found the files I needed. Besides, won't you be spending more time with a shovel than a pen now? Why, you hardly need a desk at all for your new job!"

I gritted my teeth and pushed past her before I could say or do something I would regret.

Indeed, most of my day was spent shoveling and hosing and cleaning and repeating. I walked dogs, wormed kittens, and attended to so many other inane tasks that by the time the rear end of a puppy was shoved in my face, together with the question, "Do you think his anus looks prolapsed?" it actually seemed like a normal moment.

Throughout the day, I could hear Heidi's voice, and I gave thanks for the one benefit of her incessant chatter: I was always aware of her location, and could dodge her effectively. It seemed she planned to reorganize the entire volunteer schedule in her very first shift, and I wanted no part of it.

At last, all was done for the day. I was a short distance down the road before I realized the smell of dog shit wasn't just lingering in my nostrils, I'd actually tracked the stuff into the car on my boots. I made a mental note to always bring a change of clothes and shoes to work in future.

I arrived home and found Tamara sitting on the cottage doorstep.

"Pardon my stench," I said as I stripped to my underwear right there.

Tam wrinkled her nose at the stinking pile of clothing I dropped on the lawn, then followed me inside. She closed the toilet lid and took a seat while I showered.

"The tits are going," she said once I'd pulled the curtain. "They say it's safe to do a mastectomy, provided we do it now. Anesthesia won't hurt the baby at this stage, and we can do a quick round of chemo if it's needed, then cross our fingers and toes for the duration of the pregnancy."

I stood frozen under the spray of hot water, a glob of shampoo sliding down my scalp.

What could I say?

"That's what they recommended?" I asked, reminding my fingers to move, to lather.

"Not entirely," Tam said slowly. "The mastectomy's

considered elective at this point. They'd generally do a lumpectomy and see if that takes care of it. But there's a greater risk to both myself and the baby if more treatment is needed later in the pregnancy. And I've had the testing: I've got the breast cancer gene. Howard and I talked, and we're just gonna go apeshit on this now. I mean, why the hell not? Howard's never been much of a breast man anyway."

I rinsed off, wrapped my hair in one towel and the rest of me in another, then sat down on the edge of the clawfoot tub. I leaned forward and put my hands on Tamara's knees.

"I feel helpless," I told her. "I want to fix this for you, and I can't."

"I know," she said, putting her nose to mine. "That's all that matters."

I headed into the bedroom for clean clothes and she followed me.

"Give me a hug," she said. "Howard needs to get in at least a little studio time today, and the rugrats wore Nate to a frazzle, so I think I'm up to bat now."

I hugged her, thinking in spite of myself that she felt too tiny and fragile for the battle that lay ahead. As she left, I reminded myself that she was one of the most thoroughly badass people I knew. If anyone could get through this, it was Tamara.

"I love you!" I called after her.

She startled me by popping her head back in the door.

"Stop fucking saying that like you think it's the last time I'll hear it," she scolded.

Then she smiled and chucked the bird at me and left once again.

****

The rest of the week passed in a blur.

Work was exhausting, and I couldn't decide if that was because we'd taken in a record number of animals, all of whom were now my responsibility, or because Heidi was such a ridiculous micromanager, every interaction with her was excruciating.

It took deliberate effort to count my blessings with respect to our new arrangement:

One: She appeared to be sober on the job.

Two: The board seemed to think she and I made a great team.

Three: She assigned a new volunteer, Jeff, to assist me in the mornings. He was exceptionally helpful and (petty, I know) *very* easy on the eyes.

Meanwhile, things were churning along on the home

front.

Tamara scheduled her surgery and all related appointments, then lined up child care and housekeeping as needed. She seemed to appreciate having specific tasks to focus on, and she went at them like a pitbull. Meri came over and spent a full day prepping meals designed to be super-food for both pregnancy and combating cancer. I went with Tam to yoga and tried to caution her not to overdo it. She put me in place with a single look.

Nate and Ian dove into home renovations, and together they drove Amber and Brandi to and from school each day. On Wednesday, I sat three cars behind them in the dismissal line, and watched as the girls stubbed out a shared cigarette before getting into Nate's BMW. I wondered if I should text Nate and rat them out, but decided there was no need; Ian's nose would pick up on the smell of smoke immediately.

Wolf and Kandie, meanwhile, attempted to insinuate themselves into every decision Nate and Ian faced. I received at least a half-dozen panicked texts per day from Nate, most accompanied by images of Kandie's decor suggestions. Her taste was, predictably, so appalling, I began to wonder how she'd been so unsettled by the present state of the house. I was in agreement with Nate that her suggestions could hardly be considered improvements.

Eli and Max attended their grandmother's funeral without me, as per Kitty's request. Max glided in and out of Newport with his uncle Shep, never responding to my texts suggesting we might at least meet for lunch. Eli told me he was fine, but I later overheard him telling Freya that Max had hardly spoken to him at the service.

And Finn.

Finn called and texted whenever he wasn't flying. He sounded drunk most evenings, and there always seemed to be a party going on in the background. Clearly Oklahoma was livelier than I might have guessed. I felt a distance between us that exceeded the miles, though, and I wondered if I should be concerned. We only made chit-chat in our brief conversations, partly because I didn't feel like discussing via phone some of the grave things that had transpired, but partly because I sensed he didn't want to hear anything serious anyway.

And then he was home, back at my cottage for an evening of pizza and card games with Eli and Freya. Around 10 p.m., Eli left to walk Freya to Heidi's waiting car on his way to his room at the main house. We cleared dishes and tucked the leftovers into the refrigerator. Finn pulled me into his arms. He pressed his nose into the curve of my neck and inhaled deeply.

"God, how I missed you," he said. "Did I tell you that yet?"

"Only about a dozen times," I grinned, nudging his shirt open with my nose and brushing my lips across his collarbone.

How did he do this to me, erase my doubts so quickly? Was I so damn easy all it took was a few kisses and the scent of his skin?

His hands settled onto my hips, then slid downward. He drew me to him, and the effect was the same as always: spontaneous combustion. We fumbled our way into the bedroom, shedding clothes as we went. As we fell back onto the bed, he took my face into his hands, stilling us for a moment.

"I love you, Eve," he said.

And just like that, the doubts that had crept in while he was away were banished.

"I love you, Finn," I said sincerely.

Yup.

I was just that damn easy.

Chapter **Eight**

I was dressed in black, driving to Kitty Wolcott's Newport home for the reading of her will.

To say I was nervous would be a gross understatement. I couldn't make sense of why my absence from the funeral would be required, but my presence at the reading of the will requested. It felt like a setup, though for what, I couldn't imagine. I was sweating as I handed my coat to the butler. I shook hands lightly with the Wolcott family attorneys.

Mark Fisher and John Webb may have been perfectly nice people, but in my mind, they were now and forever the pair who'd come to my husband's funeral to reveal to me the depth of his deception. I could not look at them without being transported back to the library in my former home in Jamestown, the air drawn from the atmosphere by their news. They were the messengers Kitty had looked fixed to kill that day, and now here we were, ironically enough, with Kitty gone and the two of them in charge of her estate. I settled into a chair at the edge of the room. No one made eye contact with me.

The reading of the will disclosed to me just how limited my understanding of the Wolcott fortune had been. I realized that nearly all of Skip's brothers lived or vacationed in homes Kitty had owned, and were kept afloat by the various investments Dr. and Mrs. Wolcott had made in their lifetimes. The will was so thick, its reading so tedious, Fisher and Webb took turns.

They went on…and on…and on until they'd addressed every person in the room—every person, that is, except me. All eyes turned to me as Fisher read out the final bequest.

And then, jaws dropped.

A cry went out, and a murmur rumbled among those gathered.

I was stunned.

"I… I'm sorry," I choked. "I don't think I understand."

"The remainder of the estate," he repeated, "is yours. Specifically, the family home on Ocean Drive in Newport, where we are now gathered, and the contents of…" he paused, consulting his paperwork, "...three bank accounts. I'll give you the particulars once we've settled everything, but you shouldn't worry. The net value will be more than enough to maintain the home and see the boys through the rest of their schooling. Mrs. Wolcott was insistent that there be no burden on you."

I could feel the daggers shot at me from all directions. Webb clearly noticed as well. He cleared his throat.

"Mrs. Wolcott was explicit in her final directive," he said. "She knew some of you might not understand her bequest to Eve, so I am charged with making it clear that she was of sound mind when she made this decision, and that anyone who contests her will should not only be denied their share, but will be sued for any Wolcott heirlooms in their possession. She left a detailed list of those items, and a retainer for our services, should we need to proceed. Of course, it is my hope and expectation that you will choose to respect Mrs. Wolcott's wishes."

Webb turned his attention to me. My face felt unbearably hot, and the room began to swim. I had to dip my head for a moment, but when I raised it again, John Webb remained focused on me.

"Eve, Mrs. Wolcott was not at all ambiguous in her intent. She told me personally that she felt a very special bond with you, one she did not expect her sons or other daughters-in-law to understand. In fact, she seemed concerned that *you* might not have grasped the depth of her affection for you. To that end, I've been asked to give you this letter and gift. She suggested you might like to open them in private."

A very special bond?

The depth of her affection?

I was frozen to my seat, so John Webb placed the envelope and small parcel in my hands where they lay, upturned, on my lap. The box was roughly four inches square, wrapped in black silk and tied with a black satin ribbon. The envelope was cream linen, addressed to me in the script I knew only too well from so many years of backhanded gifts on holidays and birthdays: a designer handbag because Kitty had noticed I didn't have any 'nice' ones, or a cashmere cardigan so I'd have something 'suitable' for luncheon. I stared at my name in Kitty's handwriting, and the rest of whatever Webb and Fisher had to say faded into the background.

What was Kitty's game this time? Had I really offended her so horribly that she felt the need to torment me even from the grave? What strings would I find attached to her bequest?

As soon as the library doors opened, I darted outside. I didn't dare read the letter just then, but I couldn't resist opening the package. For a split second I worried that it might be something dangerous—poison or an explosive—but then I laughed at my foolishness. Kitty was not one for overt violence. She preferred to toy with her prey.

I slipped the small jewelry box out of its wrapping and opened the lid. Even on this gloomy day, the light caught the sparkle from inside.

It was the ruby serpent brooch Kitty had been wearing the very first day I'd met her. She'd worn it to my wedding as well, and to the baptisms of my children. Its black onyx eyes were as familiar to me as the curve of its golden spine. I reached into the box and was pricked by the pin. I drew my hand back, sucking on my fingertip. I closed the lid, swallowed the metallic taste on my tongue, and set the box on the passenger seat.

I pulled my little Subaru wagon out of the drive, passing the more majestic vehicles Skip's siblings and their wives drove. I felt like the help. Or an imposter, maybe. I expected that at any moment, someone would stop me, revealing hidden cameras and confirming it was all an elaborate practical joke.

But I passed through the gates and made my way down Ocean Drive uninterrupted. The skies overhead were grey, the Atlantic black and churning madly with an early summer storm. The weather was made to order, the perfect complement to the day's events. I felt the wind take hold of my car as I crossed the bridge, leaving Newport in my rearview. My hands tensed further to steady my course. On autopilot, no doubt inspired by the trip back in time that setting foot in Kitty's house effected, I took the Jamestown exit. I found myself winding along the rocky shoreline, nearing the center of town, before what I was doing even registered.

I drove to the understated intersection where a turn in one direction would have led me to my former home. I resisted the urge to continue my trip down memory lane, instead staying the course to the public access areas at Fort Weatherill. This was a place Skip never deigned to visit. Teenagers came here to drink at night, and worse in the eyes of a Wolcott, families from Rhode Island's small, distant cities came here to fish and picnic. Common folk, lacking private waterfront access of their own. Not a demographic to which Skip could relate.

Maybe that was why I'd been coming here so long, I considered as I parked. *Maybe I always knew I was common. Maybe, on some level, I preferred to be.*

I traded my heels for the old running shoes I kept in the back of the car, then considered the wind and pulled a shabby fleece over my thin blouse. I paused for a moment, then stuffed the brooch and the letter into my pocket and zipped it shut. I hiked one of the less-worn paths toward the water. First uphill, then steeply down into the brush. Instinctively, I took care to avoid poison ivy and oak—all those things with shiny leaves of three and a painful aftermath. I slid in the gravel and dust, then emerged in the place that made the struggle worthwhile.

The wind that had rattled my car as I crossed the bridge now grabbed me, a fierce northeast gust that whipped the dust around me into a swirl that stung my eyes. Blinking against the grit, I stepped forward on the rocky outcropping. The ocean roared below, sending a salty mist to meet me. My feet found the places they'd once known well, footholds in the rock that led to a ledge where the wind would all but vanish, and feet could be dangled above the chilly spray. I sat down, pressing my back into the niche, and refastened my hair into a ponytail.

The view before me was sweeping. It was better, even, than the view from my beloved, long-lost home just a mile away. All of Newport stretched out before me, from Goat Island and the busy harbor, around the curve at Fort Adams, out to Castle Hill and the wide ocean beyond. The water was whitecapped in the wind, the scene oddly devoid of boats. Checking the weather forecast was not something I'd done lately, but clearly, mariners knew about the gusts that caught me by surprise. Far out on the horizon, a tanker cut the seascape with its dark outline, but here, close by, all vessels were moored or docked. Masts bobbed wildly in the harbor, toothpicks at this distance.

What to make of Kitty's bequest?

For much of my adult life, I'd lived as a millionaire. Had I given it much thought (and I hadn't; I'd left that all to Skip),

I'd have assumed that was the class into which we fit. Then Skip had OD'ed on drugs and infidelity, and our house of cards had come crumbling down. It had all been a charade, a lifestyle purchased on credit, reeking of default. I'd found my way forward, trading ignorance and AmEx for a checkbook balanced before each trip to the grocery store.

But while Skip had felt the need to construct a facade to impress even his own parents, Kitty's solvency was another matter altogether. It wasn't until just that day, as I sat in the library listening to the litany of holdings she'd had to offer her surviving family, that I truly understood the staggering nature of the Wolcotts' wealth.

This was no illusion, nothing like the beautiful mess Skip had fabricated. What Kitty had left to me was enough to ensure the boys could graduate high school…and college…and grad school…and more grad school with money to spare. I could buy a home to replace the one we'd lost when Skip passed. Hell, I could be the Oprah of housing: *You get a house, and you get a house, and you…!* Kitty had left me an ice-cold but pristinely maintained Newport mansion I could easily liquidate, and though I had no idea what the three bank accounts held, if it was truly enough to ensure there would be no burden on me, as Webb had said, I could only imagine it was knee-weakening.

But…

Strings.

There had to be strings.

My hand went to my pocket and was again pricked by the snake brooch. The damn thing had a life of its own. I recoiled instinctively, then reached carefully back in and pulled out the envelope that held Kitty's letter.

As if in response to that action, a particularly furious gust of wind raged, grabbing at the paper clutched in my grip and sending a spray of salt water soaring overhead. I felt my heart drop into my stomach, considering the possibility of Kitty's letter being snatched up by the wind and devoured by the sea, unread.

I jammed it back into my pocket and pulled the zipper tightly closed around it. I made my way back to the car.

There, I unsealed the letter.

Eve,

If you're reading this, you must think it is a very good day indeed. I am dead. You are wealthy. You have complete control of my grandsons' lives. I doubt you still have the bourgeois boyfriend you threw my son over for (the writing was on the wall with that one, wasn't it?), but I'm sure a woman like you won't have any trouble moving on to the next. And the next.

Because, you see, I understand you.

For a long time, I didn't think that was so. I puzzled for years over why my handsome, accomplished son chose someone as mousy and insignificant as you. He could have had anyone, but I suppose you know that. So surely, you can understand why I was baffled when he settled for you. As mothers, we simply want the best for our children, don't we? And I don't think I am telling you anything you don't already know, deep down, when I say it was clear you were not the best for Skip.

Infidelity may run in men's blood, but you pushed my Skip beyond what I'd come to accept as the norm for the Wolcott men. And then there's money, and business. The Wolcott men go together with those things naturally, yet somehow, you ruined my Skip so completely, he failed at his very birthright. I may never know all the details of what went on in your marriage, but I know enough that I can guess. You are a bottomless pit of need, and you dragged my son down with you.

I realized this the same day I realized you and I are cut from the same cloth.

You're railing against that idea, aren't you? But please, stay with me. It's certainly not a notion I accepted without a fight. After all (and let's be honest here, now that I'm a goner), I loathed you. And if you are the same as me, and I loathe you— well, why on earth would I loathe myself? How is one to make sense of that?

And then I think back, to the girl I once was. The silly thing who believed in love, who felt people could be trusted. That was what I loathed in you, that relentless clinging to such girlish notions so long after you should have grown up and known better. I saw in you the softness I'd worked so hard to beat. That weak, clinging dependence you had on medication— as if a pill could right all that was wrong with your feeble character.

And worse: you had so many opportunities that simply weren't available when I came of age. My God, you should have been ahead of the game! Yet there you were, sniveling and deferring to your husband in the very way guaranteed to alienate a man's foolish heart.

Men require management, Eve. Clear boundaries. A reminder every now and then of who truly rules the roost. But no, you couldn't manage that. You simply tottered along with the blinders on, the sort of sycophant that drags on a man like an anchor in mud.

You ruined Skip's life. Buried him in an early grave. So I want to be clear: my bequest to you is not a reward for that unforgivable behavior.

No. Quite the contrary.

Those grandsons of mine are my last hope. Eli may be

too much like you for his own good, but still, there's Max. I see so much of Skip in him. All he needs is to be nurtured in the right direction—and that requires money.

I thought of putting the money into a trust, keeping it out of your control. But once I accepted that you and I are one and the same, that simply didn't make any sense. We'd fight to the deaths for our sons, wouldn't we, you and I? And the Eve Wolcott who stood up to me that one fateful day gave me hope that you might, at last, become everything I learned to be.

Demanding.

Exacting.

Uncompromising.

I saw all of that in you that day, flashes of determination that gave me the uncomfortable sense that there might be hope for you.

And now, here we are, the two of us so alike, yet so far apart. I can see the change in you is real. Something snapped, and once that happens, there's no going back. The thread has been cut. The only question that remains is now that you've severed ties to what you were, what will you become?

And how might I help shape that change?

I'm not ill. I'm ornery enough that I may live forever. But just in case, I'm rearranging things. I'm empowering you to empower my grandsons.

I still don't like you, Eve, but now I understand you. Quelling my anger when you cross my thoughts is as simple these days as looking in the mirror.

I know you.

I know what you can become.

Don't disappoint me.

Prove yourself worthy of those handsome boys who carry the Wolcott name.

Yours.

Truly.

Kitty

****

How long did I sit there, shaking, in my car?

The sun began to set. Finally, I turned the key in the ignition and got back on the road. Though I'd promised myself I wouldn't, I went past my old house. I told myself I was going to visit Wally, my friend and former neighbor, but his house was dark. He was still in Florida, and I knew this. He'd told me he was staying this year, that he might put the Jamestown house on the market and join his senior citizen peers in what he dubbed, "God's waiting room."

I sat at the end of his driveway, looking over at the gate to my former home. The azalea I'd planted were starting to bloom. I could hear children playing in the yard. If I sat here much longer, the police would be called. This wasn't a place where those who didn't belong went unnoticed.

I pulled away and headed back toward the highway, still shaking as I glanced at Kitty's letter where it lay on the seat beside me. She'd done it, all right. No doubt, the degree to which I was upset was exactly what she'd intended.

The real question that remained, though, was whether or not she was being sincere. Did she really think she and I were cut from the same cloth, or was that just an idea she put forth for maximum impact? Kitty was no fool. She'd chosen every word she'd written carefully, the intent being to inflict the greatest possible harm.

And yet, might there be truth in it?

It would be easy to dismiss her words as the vengeance of a bitter old woman, but something in them cut so close to my greatest fears, they rang true.

You ruined Skip's life. Buried him in an early grave.

This was the sort of idea that woke me at 3 a.m. in a cold sweat. What if I'd been to blame for the sad trajectory of married life that had led Skip to his reckless behavior and untimely death? What if I'd known all along that he and I were wrong for each other, but I allowed the charade to continue? What if my spinelessness had truly cost Skip his life?

One more bridge to cross, and the wind remained strong. I fastened my grip on the steering wheel. I blinked furiously against the tears.

I made my way along.

****

"It's not a gift," Tamara said succinctly when I shared the news.

"It's her final mindfuck," Nate agreed, setting the letter down and wiping his hands as if it might have somehow contaminated him.

Howard danced behind them, his hands held high.

"The puppeteer even from the grave!" he declared dramatically.

I felt validated for how thoroughly rattled I was, yet I wasn't sure validation was what I wanted. I almost wished someone would tell me I'd misread Kitty's words.

"You do understand you are *nothing* like Kitty, right?" Tam nudged me.

I nodded, but the truth was, I wondered. I would always

wonder now. I hated that I was responding just as Kitty had surely hoped, yet what else could I do? Even if she was wrong about what I could—or would—become, there had to be a kernel of truth in there somewhere. Men like Skip had 'Oedipus complex' written all over them.

"Oh no," Nate said. "I see you drifting off there. Don't you dare give that bitch the posthumous satisfaction she was seeking."

"Okay, hush," I whispered, hearing the front door open. The rest of the crew was arriving for dinner. "I'd rather not discuss this in front of Eli. Or anyone else."

Tam, Nate and Howard all nodded in understanding. The relative quiet in the dining room vanished as Wolf and Kandie made their way in. Amber, Brandi and Eli trailed after them, and Tam and Howard's boys followed close behind.

"We brought you a special surprise!" Kandie declared. She set a massive serving tray down on the table and unwrapped it. It was piled high with deep-fried chicken parts. The smell filled the room. Tamara put a hand over her nose and ducked out into the kitchen.

"Now, I know y'all don't eat *meat*," Wolf said, "but this is *just chicken*. Kandie made it special from our restaurant recipe. One bite and you'll know why it's won blue ribbons everywhere!"

Nate leaned in and whispered in my ear, his voice a thrumming hiss.

"*Just chicken? On what planet is chicken not meat?*"

"That's so thoughtful," Howard said slowly, "but I, ah, do think chicken counts as meat, at least in my book. Haven't eaten it in twenty years! I hope you'll understand if I pass."

"It smells lovely," Nate added, "but I'm afraid I'll pass, too."

"Ian?" Kandie looked at her son, her eyes pleading.

"Um, well, Mom, I've been vegan for over a decade now, so…" His voice trailed off and his head dropped down. His shoulders sank.

A sound of disgust escaped Wolf's lips. Ian flinched as if struck.

"We'll have some," Amber said enthusiastically.

"Yes," Brandi affirmed, smiling sweetly. "We *love* to eat things that once lived!"

Each girl grabbed a pair of drumsticks and tore into them with an animalistic ferocity. They kept their eyes on Nate and Ian, looking for their reaction. Nate and Ian, however, kept their gazes downcast. They looked like scolded children.

I felt for them, but the sudden wave of nausea that gripped me took me by surprise. I fled the dining room and barely made it to the bathroom before vomiting. I knelt before the toilet, wondering if current events were taking an unusually severe toll or if I was coming down with the flu. I wasn't a fan of fried chicken, but I couldn't imagine the smell of it was enough to make me nauseous.

Tamara knocked, then pushed the door open without waiting for a response.

"Oh, baby," she said, pulling back my hair.

A shock coursed through me, and a new wave of nausea hit the pit of my belly.

Chapter **Nine**

A few days later, there was no ignoring what was going on.

There was also no blaming Kitty or fried chicken.

There they were, lined up at the edge of the bathroom sink, mocking me. Pluses and lines, pinks and blues. No matter how many times I read and re-read the various packages they'd each come in, it all meant the same thing.

I was pregnant.

Impossible, but true.

Forty.

Widowed.

Single parent to two teen boys.

And pregnant.

Knocked up.

Tin roof, rusted.

Jesus H. Christ on a motorbike, what was I going to do now?

I tried to be dramatic. With a swipe, I sent all the nasty little pee-sticks tumbling onto one another in the sink. Then, because I am nothing if not Type A, I picked them all back up again. I lined them up neatly on the edge of the vanity for a few more moments, letting the reality of the message they spelled out sink in, then I tossed them into the trash bin and closed the lid.

I sat down on the toilet seat and cried.

****

"You know I'll support you if that's really what you want to do," Tamara said. "But you also know you have to tell Finn. You can't just make this decision unilaterally."

I sat in her kitchen with teeth gritted. The iPad on the table between us was open to the Planned Parenthood site. My phone lay beside it, untouched.

"It makes the most sense," I said, swallowing a lump in

my throat.

"Eve," Tamara said gently, "I know you like for everything to make sense, but sometimes you've gotta go with your heart. Take 'sense' out of the equation and tell me what you really want to do."

I felt the tears at the corners of my eyes.

Damn you, Tam.

"I want to have the baby," I cried impulsively, "but for all the wrong reasons. I want to hit the reset button on this disastrous life of mine. I want to have with Finn what I never had with Skip—a real, true love and marriage. I want to hold a perfect little baby in my arms and have another chance at getting it right. No manipulative in-laws or boarding schools or nannies. None of the bullshit. Just a simple life. But that's crazy. Selfish. I'm forty years old. Almost forty-one. This is midlife, not a game. There's no reset button for this. And what if Kitty's right? What if I'm a horrible person, just like her? How unfair would it be to bring a baby into this mess?"

The look on Tamara's face seemed, at first, an affirmation. She was wide-eyed. Clearly she too thought I was crazy, and that going through with the pregnancy would be madness.

But then I realized she was not looking at me. She was looking past me. Over my shoulder.

I turned, and I saw Finn there in the doorway.

Frozen.

Wearing a deer-in-the-headlights look.

"Um, you weren't at the cottage, so…" he said quietly.

Tamara stood up.

"I've, ah, gotta go next door and, ah, check on Nate," she said.

I gave her a pleading look—*don't leave me!*— but she leaned in for a quick hug and then dashed off. Finn pulled out the chair next to me and sat. He put his hands on my knees and looked into my eyes.

"You're pregnant?"

I nodded.

His eyes went to the iPad.

"You're not happy about this," he said cautiously.

I raised my eyebrows.

"Finn…how could I be? I'm too old to start over. And the way things went with Skip…"

Finn pulled back. He bit his lip. Anger—an emotion I'd not often seen on his sweet face—flashed in his eyes. He stood and walked a few paces across the room, drawing deep breaths, then returned. He sat before me again, leaning in so I could not help but bring my eyes to meet his.

"Listen, Eve," Finn said quietly. "I don't intend to spend

the rest of my life atoning for another man's mistakes. But I also don't intend to spend the rest of my life without you. So we've got to work this out. Do something for me, please? Think back to the night we met. Consider what you were thinking and feeling when you chucked your wedding rings into the surf."

"I was feeling drunk," I said petulantly. "And I don't imagine I was thinking at all."

My head dipped with the lie, and I felt the weight of Finn's gaze on me. *God, he knew me.* His fingers cupped my chin and brought my eyes back to his. He peered at me, unblinking.

"I'm not asking you to tell me, not right now," he said. "Just think about it, honestly. That was a damn risky thing you did, breaking out of a life that was wrong for you, and I know you didn't do it on a whim. Years of hurt pushed you to a breaking point, I get that, but there was something else. You weren't just running *away* from something, Eve. You were running *to* something.

"You wanted something, Eve. Something for yourself. And for whatever reason, in that moment, you felt it was possible. You took the leap of faith. And I'm just nervy enough to believe it had something to do with me. Something about this connection that's existed between us from the moment we met."

I felt the tears spring to my eyes once again at his words.

I didn't bother to blink them back.

"I love you, Eve," Finn said to me, his voice softening. "Without reservation. I need you to love me the same way. Whatever is holding you back, I need you to let it go. I need you to believe we are meant to be. Think of that night. Remember what it was you wanted. And then let's make it happen together."

"Finn," I cried, dissolving into sobs as I leaned into his embrace, "I'm so sorry. I just... I worry... What if...? I'm just... I'm so sorry."

He silenced me with a kiss. I could taste the salt of my tears mingling with the sweetness of his breath. After several long moments, I came up for air, sniffing. Finn wiped at my tears with his thumbs. He put his nose to mine.

"I don't want you to be sorry, Eve," he said solemnly. "I want you to be yourself. Happily. And preferably with me."

I fell apart fully, then, collapsing into his arms.

"But what if what I want and what you want aren't compatible?" I cried. "I actually want this baby, I really do, but you always want to be off surfing and paragliding and I don't want to be alone and..."

Finn laughed suddenly.

"*That's* what you're worried about?"

I punched his chest.

"It's not funny. It's a legitimate worry!"

"Eve, those are just details. We'll work that stuff out. Our baby might even like joining us on adventures. I mean hell, I taught a cat to paddle board. I can teach a kid." He paused, kissing away my tears. His hands slipped down and rested on my belly. "You know the nice thing about being older? Nothing scares me anymore. Not even parenthood. You know why? Because the truth is, everybody fucks it up. Everybody. Hell, look at Ian and his whack-job parents. Can you imagine being raised by Wolf and Kandie? And yet he's a *mostly-functioning* adult."

I laughed in spite of myself. Finn smiled.

"Eve, we can do this any way we want," he said. "Raise this baby in Watch Hill or in a VW microbus out on the road. I don't care, as long as we do it together. You trusted me enough to jump off that cliff in South America…"

"Actually," I corrected him, "I leaned back."

"Well, yeah. And I dragged you over the edge with me," Finn noted. "So I guess we have a pattern. Brace yourself, Eve. We're going over the edge again."

I reached down, putting my hands over his on my belly.

This was madness.

Complete insanity.

But yes.

Yes, we were going over the edge again.

Happily, even.

Chapter **Ten**

JULY

Heidi and I stood in Tamara's bedroom, listening to the sound of dry-heaving on the other side of the door.

When she emerged from the bathroom, Tam was holding two things: the hair clippers she used for the boys' buzz cuts in summertime, and a clump of her own hair.

"I can't fucking take this any more," she said, her chin quivering as if she were on the verge of tears. "Help me, will you? I just want to get this over with. Be done with it entirely, and start fresh."

"Are you sure?" I asked.

"Fuck, yes," she said.

Though her word choice was typical, her voice was flat and her tone lacking in her usual bravado. I followed her back into the bathroom. Heidi drifted off, presumably to refill her bottomless martini glass.

Tam took a seat on the bench in front of her vanity. I stood behind her, and for a moment, our reflection in the mirror startled me.

My face floated above hers, the sight of the two of us together so familiar after all these years, yet so different. We were aging. How had I not noticed before? I'd noticed the lines on my own face, of course—the crinkles at the corners of my eyes, the furrow between my brows—but somehow just being with Tamara had always made me feel younger, as if some part of us remained forever college-age but virtue of our ongoing friendship.

Now, though?

Clearly age was a stealthy adversary, but there was more to it. Sickness and worry had carved Tamara's cheekbones into hollows, and her eyes lacked their usual luster. She'd made it through the mastectomy and the round of chemo intended as insurance for the coming months. Just today, she'd gotten the official word: she was, at present, cancer-free.

But the process had been brutal. Aside from a tiny,

round belly, she was rail-thin, and her hair had been coming out in clumps.

"How am I going to do it?" Tam whispered, her voice softer than I'd ever heard it. I glanced down and saw her hands, fingers spread wide across her belly. "I look like a skeleton. How can I nourish two of us for another five months?"

I felt tears spring to my eyes. I realized she was seeing what I saw, and that I'd have to work extra hard to conceal my thoughts. I rested my hands on her shoulders. I tried not to think about how slight her frame felt.

"You've got this," I told her. "The worst of it's over. It'll be a piece of cake from here on out. You're some kind of fertility goddess, totally built for this stuff."

"Not this time, I'm not," she whispered. "I don't even have boobs anymore."

It scared me, seeing Tam like this. Worse, hearing doubt edge out the boldness and sarcasm that always tinged her words. She was the strong one, and I felt ill-equipped to handle this shift in our roles.

"Dig deep," I said gently. "You have to. You'll get through this because you have to. It's that simple. You've got Howard and the boys and now this baby. They all need you. And me, Nate, my boys—all of us. What would any of us do without your badass self?" I crouched down and put my cheek to hers. I looked into her eyes in the mirror and tried to summon the tone she usually employed to pep-talk me. "You're on the upswing, okay? This is the aftermath of the battle you won. Don't forget the important part: *you won*. You beat cancer. Fuck cancer."

"Fuck cancer," she repeated. Her voice remained low, but there was a hint of her old self. She placed the trimmers into my hand. "Now shave my fucking head before I totally lose my shit."

My hands were shaking.

"My *hair*," Tamara cautioned wryly. "Take my *hair* off, not an ear."

I laughed, steadied myself, and began. Tamara's sassy short hair seemed longer as it fell away, row by row, leaving her scalp exposed. As the last of it fell onto her shoulders, our eyes met again in the mirror. I saw that there were tears making silent trails down both of our cheeks. I turned the trimmers off, placed them in her hands, and sat down on the bench beside her.

"My turn," I said.

Tamara stood up and set the trimmers down on the vanity.

"Eve, you're a doll, but don't be ridiculous," she said. "No fucking way am I letting you chop off that gorgeous hair."

"You're not *letting* me," I explained. "I'm asking you.

A little sister solidarity, like when we took that bet back in college?"

"We were drunk and broke and stupid back then," she reminded me.

"Oh, come on. It'll grow back in no time with all these pregnancy hormones, and I've wanted a pixie cut forever anyway."

Tamara shook her head vigorously. Bits of hair floated around her like snowflakes.

"Uh-uh. No way. I love you for offering, but no. I'm not gonna do that."

A gleeful cry from the doorway startled us both.

"Oooh! Oooh! I will!"

There was Heidi, sloshing vodka onto the front of her tennis sweater. She leaned against the door jamb so heavily, it was likely the only thing that kept her from becoming a puddle of alcohol and preppy on the floor.

"There!" I said, grinning. "If you won't shave my head, Heidi will."

"Oh no…" Tamara said.

"Oh, *yeth*!" Heidi slurred.

"See?" I grinned. "She's totally ready to take a power tool to my head."

Heidi nodded enthusiastically.

"I am! I've wanted to lop off all that pretty red hair ever since college!"

Tamara and I looked at each other and laughed.

"The Martini of Truth," Tam said.

Heidi nodded solemnly. She lifted her now-empty glass to her lips.

"So, who's shaving my head?" I asked. "Are you gonna woman-up, Tam, or does the task fall to the lovely lady drenched in Eau de Grey Goose?"

Tamara let out a sigh.

"I can't in good conscience let her come anywhere near you with a sharp object," she conceded, "so if you insist, here goes."

"I insist," I said, breathing deeply. I dug around in the vanity drawer and handed Tamara a pair of scissors. "Cut it as close to my scalp as possible. I think I've got enough to donate."

"You got it."

And then, with Heidi drunkenly cheering us on, Tamara went to work.

****

Finn took to calling me Annie, as in Annie Lennox.

I can't claim my buzz cut looked remotely as good as hers had back in the days of the *Sweet Dreams* video on MTV, but it was kind of him to pretend.

Tamara decided she liked being bald in the summertime, and—big surprise—Howard found the look to be a turn-on. I learned to announce my presence loudly before entering their house. Tam was feeling better every day, and she and Howard had resumed their habit of having sex any time and any place they could.

As my pregnancy progressed, I had to relinquish many of my hands-on duties at the animal rescue. Heidi found herself cleaning cat cages and dog runs, something for which she might not have forgiven me, had she not also found herself working alongside hunky volunteer Jeff. One day, I went looking for extra dog beds in the supply closet and instead found Heidi and Jeff in a position one might have described as doggie-style. I smiled and closed the door. Maybe if Heidi got laid a little more, she'd drink a little less.

Maybe.

Nate and Ian worked overtime on their house, motivated by a shared desire to be rid of Wolf and Kandie. The twins, meanwhile, allied themselves with their newly-adopted grandparents. They let Kandie paint their nails alarmingly bright colors, and they ate barbecue like rabid dogs, grinning at their

160

vegan fathers with gristle in their teeth. They attended a day therapy program, but if it was effecting change on the inside, it had yet to show on the outside. They still went everywhere with their faces screwed up in impressive scowls, their eyes nearly glued shut by gobs of mascara.

Eli and Freya took jobs at a local summer camp. They were rarely apart, and though I worried about the intensity of the relationship, I couldn't deny that it was nice to see my moody boy so happy. Max, on the other hand, spent the summer sailing in Newport with his uncles. He promised to spend the final week of the season with me, but he made it clear he wasn't happy about it. He was a Wolcott, and I was persona non grata.

One point of contention, I knew, was that Kitty's house on Ocean Drive stood empty. Title was now vested in my name, and Skip's brothers seethed over the fact. Max insisted that he should be allowed to occupy his grandmother's home. Because what teenager doesn't need a 15,000 square foot mansion?

Me—I puttered around Nana's cottage, well aware that I needed to be making some major decisions. Finn kept nagging me to move in with him in Watch Hill. He proposed marriage at least once a week. I became skilled at pretending not to have heard him, a trick I learned well from my own children. I knew I was being foolish. I was pregnant with Finn's baby. That was a lifetime commitment right there. Shouldn't I have been craving the security of marriage?

Still, once bitten, twice shy. I had only one frame of reference for marriage, and it wasn't a good one. Besides, while Finn's house was breathtaking, it didn't feel like home to me. Kitty had left me enough money to purchase a home of my own, but the funds felt tainted. I loved my work at the animal rescue, but it barely paid the bills. I could think of no clear way forward, so I just kept on treading water.

Swiftly, summer slipped by.

Chapter **Eleven**

AUGUST

"Come on," Finn called. "Are you walking with us or what?"

I stepped out of the cottage and saw that Finn had Sammie on leash, which meant a real walk, not just a meander around the paths on the property. I slipped into sandals and joined them. The sun had begun its descent toward the horizon, saturating the landscape in that late-summer afternoon glow I loved.

"You're awfully impatient today," I grinned. "Where's the fire?"

"There's something I want you to see," Finn said.

We walked up the road and I noticed there were ribbons on the fenceposts to the farm I always admired.

"Oooh—a party!" I said.

As we came closer, though, I realized there were no cars in the driveway. The gardens were in full bloom, and out behind the barn, the sunflowers would soon be in their glory. But it was oddly quiet. A few chickens pecked at the ground, but otherwise, it appeared the animals had been tucked into the barn even though it was well before sunset.

Finn paused by the fencepost. He pulled an envelope from beneath one of the ribbons, and he handed it to me. Inside, I found a set of keys—and a deed bearing my name.

"What is this?" I asked.

I knew, but I didn't quite understand.

"I figured it out," he said. "Nothing was your own in your marriage. Your husband controlled everything, and it turned out he was lying roughly 100% of the time. Then his mother tried to control you even after her death, leaving you all that money with the most brutally manipulative strings attached. No wonder you're afraid to give marriage another go. I get it.

"But here's the thing. You need a home, and I know my place doesn't feel right to you. You've got Eli here in Pinecroft, and you've got a job you love nearby. You want to stay close to

Tamara, especially after all she's been through. You've got Nate and Ian here now, too. This is where you belong. And you told me this farm is your dream home—so now it's yours."

I shook my head in disbelief.

"I don't get it. It wasn't even for sale, was it?"

"Funny thing, that," Finn smiled. "I talked to the owner one day while I was out for a run. Turns out she was looking to move to the beach. She's a record producer, and she has a friend who's a pop star with a place in Watch Hill. There was this modern house next door that she really admired, and..."

I put a hand over my gaping mouth.

"You have *got* to be kidding," I said.

Finn shook his head, laughing.

"You would think so, but no. Truth is stranger than fiction. I decided it was a sign. We worked out a trade, of sorts."

I opened the envelope once again.

"It's only my name on here," I said, studying the deed.

"Yup. You can dump me right now, and this place will still be all yours."

I looked at him quizzically. I could feel a lump rising in my throat.

"Of course, I'm kinda hoping you'll let me move in with you," he continued, "since I'm now homeless and all."

"I don't get it," I said suspiciously. "Are you trying to

buy my affection?"

"Geez, Evie, no," Finn laughed. "No matter what happens between us, I want you to know you won't ever have to worry about the rug being pulled out from under you the way it was before. You can kick me to the curb and you'll still have a place to raise our child. This is your home. Free and clear. No strings. Your salary will be more than enough for the taxes and upkeep. You don't need Kitty's money. You can cut those ties, leave that for your boys—whatever you want."

Predictably, I started to cry.

"Those better be happy tears," Finn cautioned.

I nodded.

"I think they are," I said. "I mean—it's a lot. You do realize most people don't give real estate as a gift, right?"

"You do realize most people don't have as much damn money as I do, right?" he countered.

I laughed through my tears.

"All things being relative," Finn smiled, "it's like I gave you a nice watch or something. Also, you let me knock you up, so…"

I laughed harder.

"Finn Berwick, you are *such* a romantic," I teased, punching his arm.

"And don't you forget it," he said, kissing me.

"Particularly the next time I ask you to marry me. Like, five minutes or so from now."

****

"Where's Max?" I asked Tamara, arriving in her kitchen. I held the envelope with the deed and the keys at my side. "His uncle was supposed to drop him off. I thought he'd be here by now."

She and Howard exchanged a glance.

"He was," she said.

"And he was ticked," Howard added.

Tam elbowed him.

"Ticked?" I asked.

"He expected a welcoming committee, I guess," Tamara rolled her eyes. "He was just being a teenager, you know? Moody little fucker. I think he went over to Nate and Ian's."

As if on cue, Nate and Ian came through the door.

"Have you seen the girls?" Nate asked.

Tamara, Howard, Finn and I all shook our heads.

"Max came over," Ian said. "They were in the yard talking to him, and now we can't find the three of them anywhere."

I caught the look Tam shot me. The three problem children in the family had disappeared simultaneously. This could not possibly be good.

"They can't have gone far," Finn said.

He and Ian headed in one direction. I started out toward the cottage with Tamara close behind. Nate and Howard grabbed car keys.

Barely an hour later, we regrouped on the front porch. None of us had found any sign of them, and I was officially panicked. Wolf and Kandie, who'd been ensconced in the air conditioned environs of their motor home, emerged and were debriefed. Eli and Freya joined the scene looking perplexed.

"They caught an Uber," Freya said as if stating the obvious. "To Newport."

Eli looked suddenly concerned.

"Shit, Mom, I'm sorry," he said. "I should have known that was not parentally-sanctioned."

I bit my tongue.

"I'll get the car," Finn said.

In short order, we had a caravan making its way along the shoreline. I spent most of the ride on the phone, explaining and re-explaining the situation to the Newport police. At last, I spoke with someone who seemed to understand the issue.

"The Wolcott home on Ocean Road," I said for the

umpteenth time. "I'm certain that's where they were headed. If you could just send someone to check…"

There was a pause on the other end of the line.

"We have cars on the scene, ma'am," the voice said at last.

"Scene?" I repeated.

"Yes. There's been a fire call."

My heart seized.

****

Have you ever seen a pregnant woman vault a police barricade?

Any athletic skill I lacked in high school came to me in that instant. Three police officers tried to pull me back, but I was fueled by adrenaline and hormones. Nothing—no one—could have stopped me as I ran toward the inferno that was the Wolcott mansion.

And it was an inferno.

For a split second, my mind flashed on the house as it had been when I'd first visited. I could see it looming over the chauffeured car that had carried me and Skip to the threshold two decades earlier. Now, that threshold was in flames. Flames leapt, in fact, from every window and door. The sound of glass popping and beams shattering was like fireworks, rhythmic yet unpredictable. The orange of the late summer sunset was subsumed by the eerie orange glow emanating from the Wolcott mansion. It called to mind Poe, *The Fall of the House of Usher*. It terrified me.

"Max!" I screamed. "*Max!*"

A firefighter reached out to hold me back, and I realized Nate was right behind me. He crashed into me and caught me in his arms.

And then we heard it.

"*Mom?*"

"*Daddy!*"

Nate and I ran forward in tandem. We paused as we neared the wall of flame, the heat stopping us in our tracks, and we heard the cries again.

They were coming from the carriage house.

We darted to the side and found all three of them—Max and Amber and Brandi—huddled against the side of the building. Their eyes were wide as they considered the destruction before them. They seemed, for a moment, powerless to move. They appeared to be paralyzed by fear, though if it was fear of the fire or of the absolute shitton of trouble they were certain to be in, it was hard to say.

Then the girls snapped out of their daze and rushed Nate, clinging to him for dear life. He hauled them in the direction of the barricade. Ian raced forward to meet them.

I grabbed Max by the hand and ran, never stopping until we reached safety. I wanted to slap him—I'd be lying if I said otherwise—but I also wanted to kiss him, and so that was what I did. I squeezed his face between my hands and I kissed his cheeks, and then I hugged him harder than I had in years. For the first time, he yielded. He shook and sobbed into my neck.

Beside me, I realized, another family drama was unfolding. Nate and Ian and Amber and Brandi had formed an odd huddle, clinging and crying. *"Daddy, I'm so sorry,"* was the one phrase I heard, though I didn't know which of the girls had spoken it, or to whom. To my knowledge, neither of the girls had ever called Nate or Ian "Daddy" before; it was hard to guess if this was progress, or regression to a time of trauma.

I caught sight of Kandie, who clutched Wolf's elbow and leaned into his shoulder. I followed her gaze to Ian's face, the way she studied the solemnness with which he planted a kiss on Nate's forehead and pulled the girls closer.

And there it was: the chink in the armor. A mascara-laden tear made its way down Kandie's cheek, dragging a trail through the mask of makeup shellacked onto her face. She was human, after all. A mother who cared for her child, even if she didn't have the first idea how to show it.

"Well, I'll be damned," Wolf whispered in awe. "Nate just ran right toward those flames, like it was nothing. And our Ian went right after him."

It was as if he'd broken the slow-motion spell that surrounded us. Suddenly Finn's arms were around me, and Eli was pulling his brother into an embrace. I tried to recall the last time I'd seen that.

The police began to take statements. I heard Max and the twins make sheepish admissions about booze and candles and the party they'd hastily planned. I saw Ian wave at them, indicating that they should be silent while he held on the phone for an attorney, but Nate took the phone gently from his hand, shaking his head. Without speaking, we all arrived at the decision to let our beloved juvenile delinquents face the music.

The crowd watching the disaster grew, phones and cameras held aloft. News reporters framed their shots. Lights flashed and water rained down on the Wolcott mansion from every angle, but that house was beyond salvation.

I knew what would remain in the morning: the smoldering skeleton of a thing that no longer had any place in this world.

Chapter **Twelve**

DECEMBER

My friend Tamara is always beautiful, but she's absolutely stunning when pregnant. It almost seems unfair. My skin breaks out and I feel nauseous on the best of days, depressed on the worst, and meanwhile, she positively glows. She really is some sort of fertility goddess.

This time around, there were no breasts swelling in that final trimester, and her pixie haircut was less a fashion statement and more a reminder that she'd run an unthinkable gauntlet. But there she was, stringing little white lights on a tree in her front yard, her belly occasionally impeding the task, her boys running riot around her.

The kids egged Sammie on, and my massive puppy loved every minute. He ran in circles after the snowballs they threw.

On the porch, Howard and Finn sipped winter lager and took turns queuing up music on the stereo and reminiscing about this concert or that.

Nate and Ian cozied up in one of the swings, while Eli and Freya occupied the other.

We would see the twins and Max at the tree lighting in an hour; they were volunteering in the village as part of their ongoing community service requirement.

Heidi and Jeff would catch up with us later, too. They had something they needed to take care of back at the animal shelter, they said.

Wolf and Kandie would arrive in the morning, but this time, they wouldn't be bringing their massive motor home. They'd made a reservation at the local inn. Kandie had said something about wanting to give Nate and Ian and the girls their space.

"How many pregnant ladies does it take to string lights on a tree?" I asked Tam with a grin as I offered a mittened hand.

"Tell me you're not calling us 'ladies' now," she winked.

I laughed and helped her untangle the lights.

"Are you excited for your first Christmas in your new home?" she asked.

"I am," I said. "Although honestly, I'm a little bit freaked out about what the next couple months will bring. Forty-one years old, and I'm in the home stretch of a pregnancy. Who *does* that?"

It was Tam's turn to laugh.

"Ummmmm….me? Honestly, though. When we were at Mount Holyoke, would you ever in your wildest dreams have imagined this was how our lives would turn out?"

"Never!" I said sincerely. "Never, ever, ever."

I kept my tone light, but if I were totally honest, I'd have to admit that all that had kept me going these past few months was the thought that better times must lie ahead. I couldn't be sure if it was the pregnancy or my circumstances, but I'd struggled. Daily, I had to remind myself to count my exceptional blessings.

Moving into the farmhouse with Finn had been a major transition, raising some of the ghosts of my past. Yes, legally, the house was all mine, but the knowledge that Finn had purchased it nagged at some very dark corners of my mind. Could I really consider myself independent under the circumstances? And how much independence would be enough to satisfy my troubled soul? When would I just accept that no woman was really an island?

Add to that Kitty's letter and the snake brooch. I'd let Tamara believe I had disposed of them—a sin of omission, not an outright lie—but the truth was, they sat in a safety deposit box in Westerly. I visited them now and then. The clasp on that damned brooch was most definitely broken; it always drew blood when I picked it up. And I knew the letter by heart, but somehow it seemed important to me to continue to study it. Kitty's careful script, her words so deliberately chosen—I couldn't help but think if I combed through the message often enough, I would parse out truth from manipulation. Maybe it was a delusion brought on by grief, because I was, in spite of myself, grieving. Not the loss of Kitty, to be certain, but the way her death closed a door on so much of my past.

And then there was Tamara, the sister I chose. She deserved all the happiness in the world, yet she'd been through the wringer of late, and my smaller self worried that she might not be entirely in the clear. Cancer was such an insidious enemy. Lung cancer had claimed my mother, though in that case at least I was able to point to her years of chain-smoking as the culprit. How on earth was one ever to make sense of it in Tamara's case, unless suddenly spinach smoothies and kindness were carcinogens? I was glad she'd opted for the most aggressive treatment possible, but still. Still, I loved her, and therefore, I would worry.

She smiled over at me from behind the tree, stretching to pass me the last strand of lights.

From the porch, the strains of a Paul Simon song reached my ears. I thought back to how this latest chapter in my life had begun. I could picture Tamara dancing around a suite at Ocean Manor, making up lyrics to a song that might have been entitled, *Fifty Ways to Leave Your Husband.* It seemed ages ago.

A solid drunk, a one-night stand, and the mother of all midlife crises had led me to an amazing, mind-boggling new beginning.

"Tam," I said succinctly. "Life is weird."

"Life is weird," Tam agreed. "And so are we. I'm glad you've been with me for so much of this ride."

I plugged in the last of the lights and watched the tree illuminate.

Maybe none of us ever got it all sorted out. Maybe the best we could hope for was the camaraderie of a dear friend as the years took their toll, worked their magic, and fell away.

"I've gotta tell you, sister," I said, "I feel exactly the same."

****

Later that night, I lay beside Finn, unable to sleep. Christmas candles glowed in our bedroom windows, and a fire sizzled in the hearth. Sammie dozed blissfully on his dog bed by the fire. Upstairs, I could hear Max and Eli laughing as they played a video game. I'd given up telling them to go to sleep or keep it down or any of that. I was grateful for their renewed bond. Now, when Max had school breaks, he actually seemed eager to be home. It was almost as if his accidental foray into arson had resulted in an exorcism of the Wolcott demons.

"Penny for your thoughts?" Finn inquired, and I realized he was still awake, too.

I turned to face him, and he kissed my nose. I pressed my belly into his, and he laughed when the baby moved. It had become a joke between us, the way the little alien in my tummy would leap the moment I leaned against him.

"She likes you," I said.

"You keep saying, 'she.' You peeked at that ultrasound, didn't you?"

"I didn't," I said sincerely, "but I have a feeling."

"Hmmm," Finn said. "I have a feeling, too."

He kissed me slowly, and I felt my eyes tear up. He paused, looking at me, and I saw that his eyes were tearing up, too.

Something had changed between us. We weren't courting anymore, weren't playing that game where you get to know another person, one who thrills you precisely because they are unknown. We were reaching that plateau where the thrill is a given; the connection, intense; the unknown, known. Something in Finn's eyes held me as I'd never been held before. The lightbulb went on.

This was it.

This was that indefinable *something* that had been missing all my life. Finn saw me. I saw him. And neither of us turned away.

It seemed like the perfect time, so I said the words.

"Finn, will you marry me?"

He broke the solemnity with his laugh. I considered the crinkles around his eyes, how very much I loved each of them.

"I thought you'd never ask," he said.

"Is that a yes?" I pressed.

"Oh no, Eve," he clarified. "That's not a yes. That's a *fuck yes*."

My smile grew wider.

"What, exactly, is a *fuck yes*?" I teased.

"Here," he whispered, nibbling my ear. "Let me show you."

And I let the bliss overwhelm me once again.

****

Two days before Christmas, I got the text from Tamara:

Implementing Operation New Bambino now. Existing rugrats are with Nate and Ian. Please provide backup. Don't let Wolf and Kandie deep-fry and devour my children.

I grinned and showed the message to Finn, then I replied:

Got it! Good luck—love you!!!

And then, at barely 30 weeks pregnant, I doubled over with what was clearly a contraction.

Chapter **Thirteen**

She was tiny.

Beyond tiny.

Everything about her looked more like a fetus than a baby, and my brain couldn't seem to let go of the knowledge that, had she been born in her older brothers' day, she might not have survived. I looked at her there in the incubator, her skin translucent, her eyes shielded from the light, her life dependent upon a system of wires and machines I knew nothing about, and I felt the strangest mix of emotions.

Helpless.

Frightened.

Protective.

And utterly, completely, and wholeheartedly in love.

"She's going to be fine," Finn said, pulling me to his chest and wrapping me in his arms. "You know that, right?"

"Shhhh," I whispered instinctively, patting his forearms with my hands.

I feared a jinx. My boys had both been sizable, solid, full-term babies, and even they had seemed so small and fragile to me. The extreme smallness and fragility of this new person felt treacherous and unfair. Wasn't being female in this world hard enough without being born so early that even the stability of the average newborn was something she'd have to fight for? I wanted to scoop her up and protect her, but holding her now was not an option. I'd been promised by the NICU nurses that something called Kangaroo Care—where I would hold her against me, and my bare skin would teach hers how to maintain body heat—lay in my future. But for now, we were separate.

Painfully so.

I reached a finger in to touch her, but when I saw that my index finger dwarfed her forearm, it was too much to bear. I turned into Finn's embrace and cried.

"What if she's not fine?" I cried. "She looks so...*vulnerable*."

The door to the room creaked open.

"Oh, for the love of Christmas morning. Woman-up,

Evie!"

And there was Tam. Clad in a hospital johnny and leaning heavily on Nate's arm, she shuffled in. I let go of Finn and hugged her as tightly as I could.

"God*damn*," she sighed. "I think we're getting too old for this shit. I feel like I've been hit by a Mack truck. You?"

I nodded in agreement.

"If anyone asks," Nate said, "we're your brother and sister."

"Well, you are, aren't you?" I smiled, wiping away my tears. "How's the munchkin?"

"Awesome. Howard's giving her a bottle right now," Tamara said. "He's positively glowing. Daddy's little girl, and all that, I suppose. I'm just grateful for a little more feminine energy in the house at last."

"Will they let you go home soon?" I asked.

"They tell me they're working on the discharge paperwork right now. Honestly—home birth was so much better."

Nate rolled his eyes.

"Yeah, except I'd have been lousy at performing that cesarean," he said. "I don't even know how to carve a turkey."

We all laughed. From the incubator came the smallest, saddest cries I'd ever heard.

"Hey, baby girl," Finn said, his voice tender. "We're right here."

The crying increased, her slender arms flailing at her sides.

"Hush, little darling," Nate cooed.

"Your favorite auntie is here!" Tamara added.

The crying became more furious.

"Okay, I know they said it's good that she's able to cry," I said, trying to keep my voice steady in spite of the feeling of panic rising within me, "but this seems extreme. What if she's in pain? Should we get a nurse? I don't know how to comfort a baby I can't pick up."

And just like that, the crying stopped. Her tiny eyes were covered to protect them from the bilirubin lights, but she turned her head in my direction. For a moment, she was perfectly still, as if listening, then she began to cry again.

"Wow," Finn breathed. "She knows your voice, Eve. Talk to her more."

Cautiously, I moved forward and slipped my finger in to touch her arm.

"Hey there, tiny stranger," I said quietly. "Do you know my voice? Are you the little goldfish who's been swimming around in my belly? You were supposed to stay put a bit longer, you know. Were you just too excited about coming out to play?"

Again, the crying stopped. Again, her head tipped in my direction. And when my fingertip grazed the side of her hand, she closed her fist tightly around it.

We all cried, then.

"Now who needs to woman-up, eh?" Nate asked Tamara, reaching for a box of Kleenex and passing one to his sister. She took it and elbowed him. She dried her eyes.

"Look, I hate to cry and run, but..." she said.

I nodded, gazing through my tears at my finger in my daughter's grasp. Finn dabbed at my eyes with a tissue.

My daughter.

Our daughter.

Tamara and Nate hugged Finn and kissed me, then left to prepare for Tam's discharge.

Finn moved a chair closer to the incubator. He sat down and pulled me gently onto his lap. My finger remained clasped in our daughter's tiny hand. She didn't let go.

"She's strong," I said after a while.

Finn kissed my cheek.

"Of course she is. She takes after you."

I bit my lip. The painful truth of my life was that I had never felt particularly strong, but I was trying to get better about accepting compliments and kind words. In my old life, I was never enough. It was hard to shake free of those years of training.

But this was a new beginning in respects too important to ignore. Finn and I hadn't just fallen in love—we'd brought a whole new human being into the world. She was our responsibility, and I wanted to give her the sun, moon and stars. Raising boys had been relatively easy. The world was made for them, the odds tipped in their favor. Raising a daughter would take backbone. She would have to fight twice as hard for everything she wanted, and she would look to me to be her role model. If I wanted her to be strong, I would have to be strong, too.

"I can almost hear the gears turning," Finn said. "What are you thinking, Eve?"

"It's funny," I said. "I was just thinking that, as challenging as it may be to have a baby at this stage of my life, I wouldn't have been a very good mother to a daughter twenty years ago."

"Why do you say that?"

"I didn't know myself. I was insecure. I feel badly sometimes because I think my boys felt that. Eli mirrored it, and Max rebelled against it."

Finn tipped his head at me sympathetically.

"You did the best you could in a tough situation," he said. "You do know you're human like the rest of us, right?"

I smiled and nodded.

"I do. I guess what I meant is that I'm grateful she came to us now. I feel like a different person. Tougher. More experienced. And I think daughters need that."

"I'd been thinking throughout the pregnancy that this feels like a second chance," Finn said, and I knew he was referring to Molly, the daughter who'd grown up without him. He nodded his head at the baby sleeping calmly now in the incubator. "But look at her. As small as she is, she's her own person, and a fighter at that. It's not really about another chance for you or for me, is it? It's about her—her dreams, her adventures. I'm glad you and I are both older and wiser now, mostly because I think we're going to have one hell of a time keeping up with her."

I laughed. I felt the grip on my finger relax, then tighten again. Maybe Finn was right.

A nurse knocked, then opened the door.

"We have a situation," he said.

My heart sank, and he seemed to realize he'd chosen his words poorly.

"Oh no, no—not a medical situation. But we can only let immediate family into the NICU, and it seems you have, ah, an *unusually* large family. Could you come with me?"

I reluctantly extricated myself, gently wiggling my

finger free. Finn helped me back into the wheelchair and we followed the nurse down the hall.

"You'll have to scrub in again afterward," he reminded us, opening a door.

"Merry Christmas!"

The chorus of voices nearly overwhelmed me.

The small lounge off the NICU was packed. Eli and Freya ran forward to hug me. They were wearing matching sweaters, and I guessed I'd missed out on some sort of Christmas-gift joke. Max hung back at first, giving an awkward wave, then he stepped up and kissed my cheek. Ian and Wolfe shook hands with Finn, and the twins mumbled, "Congratulations" in somber unison. Howard kissed my cheeks at least a dozen times, while Kandie delivered air kisses from a distance. Howard and Tamara's boys appeared to be building a fort out of furniture in the far corner of the room.

I spotted Tamara on a sofa, looking a little nervous as Heidi cradled her new baby. Jeff sat beside them, and I didn't miss that Kandie seemed to be keeping watch on him out of the corner of her eye. I guessed our self-proclaimed Florida cracker girl was getting a lesson in diversity from Heidi's tall, dark, handsomely dred-locked amour.

Finn wheeled me over.

"I thought you were going home," I said to Tam,

grinning.

"We are," she said. "Truly. I can't fucking wait to get out of this place. But since you can't come to Christmas dinner, this crew decided to bring Christmas dinner to you."

"You'll just have to forgive us," Ian said, indicating the selection of cafeteria food on trays at the center of the room. "This was about it for options today."

"But there are LOTS of veggies!" Kandie proclaimed brightly. "Since we know y'all are weird about *real food*."

I caught the smile that passed between Ian and Nate. Everyone began digging in.

Heidi passed Tamara's baby over to me, and I marveled at how large she seemed compared to my tiny bundle of joy. And Tam had been so afraid she wouldn't be able to produce a healthy baby! I smiled at my friend and realized she looked healthier than she had in a long while. It was as if her baby wasn't the only one who'd been gifted with new life.

"Can you believe it?" Tamara mused. "Both of us, here and now, giving birth to daughters? Truth is stranger than fiction."

Heidi took a long slurp from a mug I suspected held something stronger than coffee.

"Doesn't surprise me," she said. "You are both absolutely insane. Have been ever since college." Tamara and I laughed.

"Absolutely," I grinned. "And we'll get to raise our wild and crazy daughters together."

Finn came over and peered at the swaddled bundle in my arms.

"Does she have a name?" he asked.

Howard put an arm around Tamara. He was, in fact, glowing.

"Grace," he said.

"That's perfect," I sighed.

I felt a hand on my shoulder and turned to see the nurse.

"We've arranged a viewing, if you and your guests would like to head to the window."

Eli and Freya pulled back the curtains along one wall. There, on the other side of the glass, was the incubator and its miniature occupant. The sighs in response were immediate, with a couple of notable exceptions.

"Eeew—it looks like a fetus!" Amber said.

"Or an alien," Brandi added.

Nate and Ian shot them withering glares.

I laughed and said, "She kind of does, doesn't she?"

"Well, a *cute* fetus," Amber backpeddled diplomatically.

"And she's not nearly as ugly as most aliens," Brandi conceded.

"Right—'cause you've seen how many aliens?" Max snarked.

"Well, you know," Brandi pouted. "In movies and, like, Netflix and stuff."

"Hey, wait a minute!" Tamara said. "Does *she* have a name?"

Finn looked to me.

"Hope," I said. "Her name is Hope."

The room grew quiet.

"Perfect," Howard said, nodding.

And then, before the moment of silence that descended could get too heavy, Tamara looked from her daughter to mine.

"Grace and Hope. Good thing we're not burdening these kids with too many expectations, eh?" she winked.

****

Later that evening, Finn slept on the sofa while I sat in the chair beside the incubator. Max and Eli had both texted to ask how their little sister was doing, and I wondered if Tam had put them up to it. They genuinely seemed curious, though, as if they were drawn in by this new twist in their family story. Molly, meanwhile, had called Finn—to hear about the baby and to share news of her own: she'd been accepted to Brown, early-decision. She'd be heading to Rhode Island for college.

I thought about all the strange ways life had of falling apart and then coming back together. There had been so much change in the lives of everyone I loved. Deaths and births. Cancer and remission. Adoption and adaptation. Moving house and healing relationships. Learning and growing and moving on. Forming families in ways none of us might ever have imagined.

Now, my eyes were fixed on Hope.

In a way, I felt I'd known her forever. That part of me had been waiting for her. There was something about her slight form that made me feel the accident of my pregnancy was no accident at all. My initial worry at her frailty had already turned to wonder: *who would she grow up to be, and how might she change the world?*

Was it just a mother's love, this odd certainty that the impossibly small human sleeping before me, tethered to medical equipment for the sake of her very life, would grow to do great things?

Finn yawned and shifted.

Hope sighed.

All around us, machines beeped steadily as a metronome, and out in the hallway, there was the occasional murmur of voices. Somewhere, very faintly, I heard the strains of *Silent Night*.

Truth is stranger than fiction.

I knew I should get some sleep, but I felt strangely awake.

Wired.

Stirred by a story I wanted to tell.

I dug in my bag and found my notebook. I turned to a clean sheet of paper. I chewed on the end of my pen for a moment, humming.

I wrote a title tentatively at the top of the page, then crossed it out and tried again:

FIFTY WAYS TO MAKE A FAMILY

Yes, I had a story I wanted to tell. I had no idea if it would be something I would share with the world, or just tuck away for my daughter to read when she was grown. But there was a story that had taken root in the strangest of ways, a series of events that had come to pass when I'd felt I couldn't go on.

And weren't those always the best kinds of stories, the ones where the new beginning came from what had seemed to be the end?

ACKNOWLEDGMENTS

This book had more false starts than I can count. It truly might never have seen the light of day if not for the incredible journey I undertook this past year with the support of so many.

A wholehearted thank you is due...

To Julianna Ricci, whose coaching sent me off on the adventure of a lifetime.

To Ron Kohn, who introduced me to paragliding more than a decade ago, and kept both me and the love of it alive long enough for this story to emerge.

To Jeff Kelley: our connection alone was worth the journey to Humboldt. In wind and rain and occasionally kinder weather, we walked and talked, and it turns out that sometimes a musician is exactly the kind of creative soul who most inspires a writer. *Never been done*...but it will be.

To the ladies of Wednesday Girls' Night Out, who instantly made me feel at home on the West Coast and gave me a sense of community—I cannot thank you enough. To find a safe space where people truly do not judge is nothing short of a miracle.

To everyone at the noon meeting, who welcomed me in at my lowest, raised me up higher than I imagined I could go while sober, and were there for the roller coaster ride all along. Y'all impress the hell out of me, and I love you. (A special shout-out to my road trip buddy Mike. xoxo)

To the thriving arts community in Humboldt: Director Roy King and everyone at Westhaven Center for the Arts, Bayley Brown at KHUM, the fabulous OLLI community at HSU, Lauraine and Jack at Mad River Union, and so many more. Considering all the creativity among the redwoods, it is no surprise to me that it was there that I was finally able to wrap this baby up.

To Steve and Karen and all my coworkers at Trinidad Bay Eatery and Gallery: thank you for the absolute best summer job ever. You kept me well-fed and highly amused while leaving me the requisite mental energy for writing. There cannot possibly be a harder-working, more dedicated group of people anywhere. (Also: I apologize for nearly burning the place down with those forgotten cookies. And if you didn't already know about that…never mind…)

To my dear long-distance friend Brea Brown, whose talent and drive as an author inspires me, and whose wit and kindness have sustained me in some dark-night-of-the-soul moments these last few months. Brea, I doubt you know how much your friendship means to me—so I'm putting you on notice here. Thank you so much for everything. Ditto for Martha Reynolds—I miss our coffee-and-conversation meetups, but I'm grateful we can stay connected through social media.

To Gary McCluskey, who has once again provided me with an AMAZING cover—and plenty of snarky, irreverent conversation about the, ahem, *joy* of being creative.

To my friends and family who made sure the anchor held fast back East while I went off on my Wild West adventure: I know how lucky I am to have you in my corner.

To my sister Kristen McDonough—an extra debt of gratitude for your willingness to share your NICU experience, and to my delightful, vivacious niece Addie, thanks for serving as the inspiration for Hope.

To the research assistants at Dana-Farber Cancer Institute who steered me in the right direction for answers to some very difficult questions.

To my son Ryan, who has patiently weathered my ongoing midlife crisis and supported my growth as a person, even when he clearly thinks I am nuts. *You're the best, Pokey, and you are indeed a grown-ass man.*

And to Mario, whose kind, gentle heart makes me feel my faith in love is not misguided, and that telling tales of romance is not a foolish business. That someone I respect so deeply champions my success is no small thing. Thank you for all the adventures, from Lost Coast to Heart Lake and everywhere in between. You are wacky, and that is good.

Here's to many, many more adventures ahead.

Much love,

K.C.
Mount Shasta, CA
December 2016

ABOUT THE AUTHOR

K.C. Wilder is the author of the bestselling novel *Fifty Ways to Leave Your Husband*, the Heather Hollow series of YA paranormal fiction, and the novella *Seattle Postmark*. Her short fiction appears in the compilations *Wrecks*, *A Kind of Mad Courage*, and *Merry Chick Lit*. She is a contributor to Elephant Journal and The Huffington Post, and she blogs weekly about women, adventure and creativity at Girl on a Wire.

Connect with her at **www.girlonawirekcw.com**

CRAVING MORE OF THE *50 WAYS* CAST OF CHARACTERS?

Coming in 2017: three novellas full of juicy details—your favorite secondary characters in lead roles, telling their own stories…

Here's a sneak peek:

DOUBLE NEGATIVE
a *Fifty Ways* novella
by k.c. wilder

FINN

There they are in the same room: the daughter I never really knew, and the one who's just entered this world far too early. Eve has Hope tucked against her chest, and she's explaining Kangaroo Care to Molly. The warmth of Eve's skin, the sensation of her heartbeat and breathing—these things train our preemie's tiny body to do what full-term babies' bodies do naturally.

There's more to it, though. When she is in Eve's embrace, something about Hope changes in a way I don't think all the wires attached to her can measure. It's as if she knows she and Eve were supposed to remain connected still, and these sessions are a homecoming.

I have the sense that it's different when I hold her, and I'm not sure if that's something I've made up in my mind, or if it's true. It scares me, frankly, to love such a small, fragile stranger so much.

Now Molly's here, flown in for a quick visit. Later today we'll head over to the East Side, check out the Brown campus now that we know it will be her school. I'll buy her a sweatshirt at the book store, maybe. That's what parents do, right?

And I will try—really, really try—to honor Dani's wishes. To keep being Uncle Finn in spite of this weird awakening of paternal instincts Hope's arrival seems to have inspired. I catch myself looking at Molly too often, wanting to apologize to her for my absence as she grew.

But I can't.

Of course I can't.

Molly's biological father is supposed to be dead and gone.

MOLLY

He's supposed to be my uncle. Do they think I was born yesterday? Looking at Finn is like looking into a mirror.

I don't know what went on between him and my mom, and I can't even begin to process all the lies at the center of my childhood, but I'd bet my near-perfect SAT scores on one thing:

Finn Berwick is my father.

DOUBLE JEOPARDY

a *Fifty Ways* novella

by k.c. wilder

HOWARD

"Don't you dare fucking cry," she warns me.

I've spent the better part of the past twenty years dealing with her false bravado. For the most part, I'm used to it. Tamara's verbal barbs roll off me like water off a proverbial duck's back. This time, though, I find myself so irritated, I want to shake her.

"Don't you dare fucking tell me what to do," I retort.

Both of us are shocked.

"Howard, I..." she begins.

I shake my head, wanting anything but words, and I reach out and take her hand.

Tamara is my life. I can't even pretend that ours is a healthy relationship. If you look up 'codependent' in the dictionary, I'm pretty sure you'll see our picture. We'd make one hell of a psychological study.

And yet, I don't care.

All I care about right now is making sense of the diagnosis that doctor just delivered with all the emotion of a person placing an order for takeout.

Cancer.

And pregnancy.

Apparently, these things do coincide often enough that there is protocol for dealing with them. It boggles my mind. It's like finding out there are layers to this world you never imagined existed. This is someone's job, dealing with things like this on a daily basis. And that someone just left us in his office so we could "have a moment."

We are, indeed, having a moment.

"It's okay," Tamara tells me now, her voice much quieter. "You heard what he said. It's early enough that, even with aggressive treatment, the baby should be fine."

I snap then.

"I don't care about the baby," I spit out.

Tamara pulls her hand from mine as if she's been stung.

"You love babies," she says.

"I love *you*," I whisper.

And then, against my wife's wishes and utterly without a choice in the matter, I cry.

DOUBLE EDGE

a *Fifty Ways* novella

by k.c. wilder

THE TWINS

She peered out the window, then wheeled around to face her twin.

"Are you kidding? Those *losers*—that's what we get? A couple of khaki-wearing, fudge-packing pinheads?"

"Have you forgotten?" Amber hissed. "It's been eight years since anyone was *remotely* interested in adopting us. Those *losers* are our last hope."

"Well," Brandi sighed, "at least if they're queer they won't be trying to crawl into bed with us."

"Exactly. And I saw their car. It's a BMW. What's the rule?"

"Always look for the silver lining."

"Amen, sister. Always. Now give it up."

Amber held out her hand. Brandi spit her chewing gum into her sister's open palm, then stuck out both her tongue and her middle finger.

"Keep it up and your face will freeze that way," Amber cautioned.

"Nineteen minutes," Brandi reminded her. "You've only got nineteen minutes on me, so quit acting like you're my mother."

"If ever anyone needed a mother..." Amber rolled her eyes. "Tug down the hem of that skirt. You look like a slut. Queer dudes won't adopt a couple of sluts. They need us to make them look normal."

"Unless they're pimps," Brandi gasped. "Oh my god— *what if*? Remember that episode of CSI..."

"Shhhhh! Here they come." Amber reached out and yanked her sister's dangly earrings from her lobes and stuffed them into her pocket. She licked her thumb and smoothed her hair back from her temples. "Remember..."

"I know, I know. Sweet as apple pie. Got it."

They turned and flashed their megawatt smiles at the pair of men who flanked the social worker. The ultra-slim, balding guy looked too nervous to speak. The other one— blond and bit stocky—put out his hand. Brandi wouldn't have admitted it to Amber, but there was something she instantly liked about his smile. He was the human equivalent of a golden retriever.

"Hi," he said. "I'm Nate, and this is Ian."

www.girlonawirekcw.com

·

Made in the USA
Middletown, DE
12 December 2016